I0729331

THE AMAZING MASTER DAVIEL AMBERSTCROMBIE

IN

The Mystery of Crescent Hook Island

BOOK 1

By Daniel S. Wyckoff, Sr.

Copyright © 2022 by Daniel S. Wyckoff, Sr.

The Mystery Of Crescent Hook Island

ISBN-13: 978-1-7346566-2-6

All rights reserved. No part of this book may be reproduced, stored, or transmitted by any means - whether auditory, graphic, mechanical, or electronic - without written permission of both publisher and author, except in the case of brief excerpts used in critical articles and reviews. Unauthorized reproductions of any part of this work is illegal and is punishable by law.

Table of Contents

CHAPTER 1
THE ELDERLY WOMAN

"Hey you, kid, get back here!" yelled the elderly woman.

Daviel (Dah-v-el) turned to see who was yelling, and at whom.

"Yeah, you kid," screamed the woman looking at him.

Daviel turned again to see who had passed him but no one was there. "Who, me?" he asked.

"Well, I'm not talking to the sidewalk," said the woman sarcastically. "Get back here."

Daviel shrugged his shoulders and walked back to the raving woman. "How may I help you?"

"Don't try and sweet talk me kid; I saw you," said the woman.

"Saw me? I was standing right over there," he said with a confused expression on his face.

"Don't be so impertinent," snapped the elderly woman. She stared at him for a few minutes before asking, "Well, what do you have to say for yourself, young man?"

"About what ma'am?" he asked. Daviel was always polite and said "ma'am" and "sir".

"Don't you go saying ma'am to me," she said in a somewhat quieter voice.

"Yes ma'am, I mean no ma'am, I mean...."

"Say what ya mean boy and get on with it," snapped the woman.

The woman's yelling attracted the attention of a police officer. "Is something wrong Leti?" he asked, eyeing the boy curiously.

"Wrong you ask? What I want to know is: where were you when all this happened?" scolded the woman.

"What happened?" officer Johnos asked Daviel.

"Don't ask me," he said shrugging his shoulders. "I was standing over there minding my own business when she started screaming. When I turned to see who was yelling, she yelled at me to come, so I did." he explained quickly not pausing to take a breath.

"What happened you ask — what happened — look at that, that's what happened? Look at my hat, look at it!" she said pointing to what she was holding in her hand.

Daviel and Officer Johnos looked at each other, then at the thing in her hand.

That is a hat? thought Daviel.

It was obvious to the woman that Officer Johnos was not going to be any help. Slowly she explained, "I saw this boy throw my hat in that garbage can over there. That's what happened. First he destroyed it and then he threw it away!"

Officer Johnos tried to hide his smile as he turned his head to look at the boy. "What do you have to say for yourself, young man?" he asked in as serious a voice as he could.

"Uh, um," stuttered Daviel somewhat perplexed. "I was walking down the sidewalk and I saw something lying in the street," he explained. "I went and picked it up. I thought it was garbage, so I threw it away."

Turning to the woman he said, "I am sorry ma'am. I did not realize it was a hat."

"Humph," snorted the woman. "No respect for other people's property. That's what's wrong with you boys today. 'Sorry' you say, and I bet you expect me to forgive you for destroying my hat and then throwing it away for me." Looking at Officer Johnos she said, "Sorry he says."

Turning back to Daviel she said, "I paid a dollar fifty for this hat, young man. Money don't grow on trees you know."

"Yes ma'am, I mean no ma'am, I mean…."

"There you go again," said the elderly woman. "Boy, you can't even talk proper. Now what are you going to do about my hat?" She asked Officer Johnos.

"I'll buy you another one Leti," soothed the officer.

"Oh, no you won't," Leti objected. "This here young man destroyed it and he'll have to pay for it," she said looking down her nose at the confused boy.

"I am sorry your hat was destroyed ma'am," started Daviel.

"Sorry! Sorry, don't buy me no new hat!" yelled the woman. "Yer wouldn't have to be sorry if ya hadn't of destroyed it in the first place. Didn't yer ma teach you not to touch other people's property?"

"But ma'am," protested Daviel. "I did not destroy your hat. I only found it lying in the street and threw it away."

"Likely story," exclaimed Leti turning to officer Johnos. "Well?" she demanded.

Officer Johnos was perplexed as to what to do. It was Leti's word against the young man's. Looking at the young man he saw a clean-cut youth about thirteen years of age. Actually, Daviel was almost fifteen. He was wearing good clothes and even his shoes were polished. The boy's dark red hair was thick and wavy, not curly, and his eyes were emerald green. Amazingly he did not have the light white skin of normal red heads and there were no freckles. He was a good-looking boy who stood about five feet five inches and he guessed that he probably weighed no more than one hundred twenty pounds. He could not imagine this boy vandalizing another person's property.

Turning to Leti he said, "Let me speak privately to the boy."

As Leti entered her home officer Johnos asked kindly, "Where are you from, son?"

"I live over on Baskell street sir," explained Daviel.

Officer Johnos knew where that was and also knew that it was in the rich section of town. All the homes in that area cost a minimum of five hundred thousand dollars.

Daviel continued, "My parents were killed in a car accident so I live with my guardians, Judge and Mrs. McKnight."

Judge McKnight, thought officer Johnos, is a very powerful man.

"Uncle James was supposed to be my guardian but —"

"Why wasn't Uncle James made your guardian?" interrupted officer Johnos. "Why don't you live with him?"

"He was my dad's best friend and my dad wanted him to be my guardian and for me to live with him, but he was going through some difficulties so he declined and Judge McKnight became my guardian. I will gladly buy the lady a new hat even though I did not destroy hers. I, well, I am very rich," stammered Daviel.

Officer Johnos pondered, "No, I do not believe you destroyed Leti's hat. However, what are you doing in this section of town? It is not exactly the best area you know."

The street where Daviel and Officer Johnos were standing was in "the projects." The tenement houses were all run down and in desperate need of repair. Leti's house was one of the better ones on the street but it too desperately needed some help. Since this was a main street through this section of town it was clean but Daviel could see the trash piled up on all the side streets.

Smiling Daviel answered, "No it isn't. I met a boy a little younger than me the other day. He was hit by a car and I helped him get to the hospital. I went by there today to check on him but the nurse told me that he had already left. She gave me his address so I took a taxi here."

"What's the boy's name?" asked officer Johnos.

"It was Drew, Drew Smite," said Daviel.

"Drew was about your age you say?"

Daviel nodded his head yes and then added, "He is probably a little bit younger than I."

"I'm sorry, but there is not a boy named Drew living on this block. What did you say was his last name?"

"Smite, I think," replied Daviel.

"Smite," repeated the officer. "Wait a minute, could it have been Smythe?"

"I guess so," responded Daviel.

"Ah, Andrew Smythe," said the officer chuckling to himself.

"What is so funny?" asked Daviel.

"Um, Drew is Leti's grandson. Come on," he said knocking on Leti's door.

"Well?" asked Leti opening the door.

"This young man," replied officer Johnos, "has come to see Andrew."

"Andrew," stammered Leti. "What do you want with my grandson?" she asked.

"It seems," said the officer, "that this is the young man who helped your grandson the other day when he was hit by a car."

Leti was shocked and embarrassed at the same time. "You're, you're the one?" asked a surprised Leti.

"Yes ma'am, I guess I am," replied Daviel.

"Come in, come in," she said in a sweet voice. "Drew has done nothing but talk about the young man who helped him. He will be so excited to see you. Drew, you have company!"

"Who is it grandma?" yelled Drew from his bedroom.

"Just hold your horses boy, we're coming."

Turning to Daviel she said, "I hope you will forgive a foolish old woman. I know you could not have destroyed my hat. Please forgive me."

"Yes ma'am, however I would like to buy you another one."

"Truthfully I never did like that ugly old hat so don't worry about it."

Again, Drew called from his bedroom.

"Have some patience boy, I'm not as young as I once was, you know."

Leti and Officer Johnos entered the room blocking Daviel from view.

"Hi Officer Johnos, thanks for coming to see me."

"Actually, I was coming to see you Andrew but I'm not the surprise visitor." Stepping aside he let Daviel enter the room.

"It's you, it's really you!" shouted the excited boy.

"It is I," said the smiling Daviel. "I went to the hospital to see how you were doing and they told me that you had already checked out. The nurse gave me your address." Turning to Leti he said, "I hope ma'am that was all right."

"Of course, it is, young man."

Daviel visited with Drew for about an hour and then left for home. During the taxi ride home, he was deep in thought. He was surprised at the condition of Drew's house. The paint was peeling from the walls, the carpet was threadbare, and Daviel knew that when winter came it would be very cold. The furniture seemed to be of good quality. He realized that something must have happened that made them move to this area of town.

He wanted to help but how could he help Drew and his grandmother? He believed that the Lord had given him his wealth to help others. As God brought people across his path he would try to help as many as he could.

Being rich, he was in a financial position to help others but sometimes being rich without having the knowledge of how to handle money can cause problems.

Thinking back in time ….

CHAPTER 2
DAVIEL LEARNS A LESSON

"Wake up sleepy head," said Mrs. McKnight. "It's time for breakfast. School starts today."

"Oh," groaned the small boy. "Do I have to go?" He asked.

"Come on sleepy head. You don't want to be late your first day."

Mrs. McKnight was the perfect picture of the perfect grandmother. She was fifty-two years old with wavy grey hair, green eyes, and still had a beautiful complexion. She was the envy of all her friends. Most grandmothers are somewhat portly with wrinkles, but not Mrs. McKnight. She was five feet two inches tall and weighed one hundred and five pounds.

Everyone adored her. She was always smiling and cheerful and willing to help anyone in need. When her husband came home and told her about the twelve-year-old boy in his court room and that he wanted them to become his legal guardians she readily agreed. After having Daviel for two months she deeply loved the small boy.

Daviel, at thirteen, was a small boy who actually liked school; however, this year he was starting middle school and that meant P.E. and P.E. meant taking showers. Being small for his age and an only child made taking showers with other boys his age a new experience for him — — one that he would rather not have. The other problem was that being small for his age he was not overly excited about all the older, bigger boys in middle school. How would they treat him? He had heard stories about the older boys picking on the younger ones, even in a Christian School. He had heard that….

"Daviel," called Mrs. McKnight interrupting his thoughts. "If you do not hurry young man you will have to go to school without breakfast."

To Daviel, who enjoyed food, that was almost worse than going to middle school, but not quite.

"*Buck up,*" he told himself. "*It cannot be all that bad.*" He thought, "*What is the worst that can happen?*" He would soon find out.

Judge McKnight, Daviel's guardian smiled at the boy. "Nervous," he asked?

"Yes sir."

The judge patted the boy on the shoulder. "It will be all right. Soon you will be making new friends and having a great time." As an afterthought he said, "You know that if you have any problems I'll help you."

"Thanks," replied Daviel, but he was thinking, *"Great! That is all I need, the judge coming to school to defend me. I would really be a freak then."* Being extremely smart caused him enough problems.

Daviel had no intention of ever letting the judge know if he had any problems. He would handle them himself. Daviel had been living with the McKnight's for two months since his parents had died. The judge and Mrs. McKnight were really nice and were very good to him. They were busy people though and did not have a lot of time to give him and besides that, they were old.

Judge McKnight retired from the bench at the age of fifty-five. Daviel's case was the last case that he heard.

After becoming foster parents to Daviel he decided that he wanted to do other things with his life and after spending twenty-eight years on the bench it was time to retire while his health was good. Everyone who knew him was shocked when he retired especially since he was up for the Supreme Court nomination.

Judge McKnight was known as the compassionate judge. Standing six feet with grey hair, wire rim glasses, and brown eyes, he was always smiling. He weighed one hundred and eighty pounds, exercised daily, and ate a healthy diet. He was well respected amongst his peers and everyone loved him, everyone except for the criminals. He never let his compassion for others override his good judgment.

Criminals feared him, not because he was mean, but because he upheld the law. His motto was "If you do the crime, then you do the time." After seeing the small boy in his courtroom his heart went out to him and he and his wife became his legal guardians.

"Do you want me to go in with you," asked the judge as he pulled in front of the school.

"Thanks, anyway, but I can take care of myself."

Slowly the boy got out of the car and entered the building. At the last minute he turned and waved to the judge. He knew where his homeroom was. He and Mrs. McKnight stopped by last week to pick up his class schedule. The middle school only occupied two floors of the building so finding the rest of his classes would not be a problem. He already knew where the dreaded gym building was.

Since he was one of the last to arrive, he had to sit near the front. That was fine with him. At the front no one would bother him, he hoped. A few minutes later his teacher entered.

"Good morning class, my name is Mr. Atkins. I will be your home room teacher and your math and science teacher. Please answer here when I call your name."

After the roll was taken and the announcements made the teacher called several boys up to his desk, including Daviel.

"Boys," said the teacher, "we had to make some schedule changes so here are your new schedules. We are sorry for the inconvenience."

The bell rang for first period. With a little fear he looked at his new schedule. As he was looking at it the boy beside him yelled, "Whoopee!"

The boy was a little bigger than Daviel but not much. He smiled at Daviel, "I now have P.E. for last period so I won't have to take a shower before going home," he explained with a slight blush.

Daviel looked to see what he had for last period. Could he be as lucky as the other boy? With a big smile he saw that he too had P.E. for his last period.

While Daviel was checking out his new schedule the other boy went on to his class. When Daviel entered his class room, he spied the young man sitting at the back of the room. The boy motioned for him to take the seat next to him. As he sat down they compared their class schedules. They had all the same classes except Daviel had art when the other boy had band.

"My name is Daviel, what is yours?"

"My name's Harold but everyone calls me Hal. It's nice to meet you."

Before the boys could say any more the class started. Hal too was small maybe a half inch taller than Daviel. With straight black hair and blue eyes, the girls thought he was very good looking. Everyone who knew him thought he should be a movie star.

The boys talked off and on during the day, especially at lunch. They learned that they were both thirteen and were both born in July. Hal was only three days older than Daviel. Both were only children and both dreaded having to take showers at school.

The day passed quickly for the two new friends. They really enjoyed being in the same classes. For Daviel, who never had a best friend before, this experience was exciting. Maybe, he thought, Hal and I will become best friends!

"Well," said Hal, "only one more class for the day. It has gone a lot better than I had feared."

Smiling at his new friend Daviel said, "It sure has. I was afraid the bigger boys would pick on me since I am so small. He —" he started to say something when someone said,

"Do you boys think you might like to join the class?"

"Sorry," they called, running to the gym.

"Sorry we are late, sir," said Daviel. "We were talking."

"So, I see," said the smiling coach, "I will excuse you this time but if it happens again you will have to run extra laps around the gym."

"Thank you, sir," said the boys in unison and Daviel added, "We will not be late again sir."

The coach was a big man. Daviel and Hal had to look up at him. He stood a little over six feet, was broad shouldered, and very athletic looking. Blond haired, and blue eyed, he was the idol of many a young boy. Of course, the fact that he really was nice helped. His only desire was to help boys develop into the men they could be, both physically and spiritually. During his teaching career many a boy had looked at him as a second father. Besides giving good, godly advice, he was a real friend too!

Coach explained what he expected of the boys. He believed in physical exercise and said he expected all the boys to always do their best. He went on to explain that he knew that each boy was different and that some would have more physical abilities than others but everyone would be expected to work hard.

Daviel considered himself to be physically challenged though he actually was well coordinated and athletic. He really did not care for sports of any kind, but he would do his best. When P.E. class was finished most of the boys got undressed for showers. Daviel, Hal and another boy changed into their regular clothes.

The first week of school had gone by quickly and without any problems for Daviel or Hal. They were on their way to becoming best friends. Daviel and Hal were talking during lunch when a couple of bigger boys came by.

"What do you have in that sack kid," one of the boys asked Hal.

Hal and Daviel ignored him hoping that he would go away.

"Hey little boy, are you deaf. I asked you, what do you have in that sack?" Then he grabbed the sack out of Hal's hand.

"Hey," yelled Daviel, "that's not yours, give it back to him!"

The older boys' friends told Daviel to be quiet; his turn was coming. The other boy took out Hal's sandwich and started eating it.

Hal grabbed his sandwich, his lunch bag and ran. Some of the boys ran after him until they saw a teacher enter the lunch room. One of the boys whispered to Daviel "Later squirt."

The rest of the day Daviel and Hal kept looking over their shoulders but they never saw the boys again. Feeling relaxed as they waited for their rides home Hal asked Daviel where he lived.

After Daviel told him, he heard someone say, "That's a nice section of town squirt, a real nice section."

The two friends turned around. The bullies were right behind them. As they started to run the bullies grabbed their shirts.

"Hold on partner," said one of the bullies, looking Daviel in the eye. "I suppose living in that area of town you must get an allowance."

Daviel did not answer.

"I'll take that as a yes. Now squirt, here's what you're gonna do, unless you want to get your head bashed in by one of the boys," he said grinning at his friends. "You will bring me five dollars a week for protection money. Every Monday you will pay me five dollars as a protection fee and the boys and I will protect you from the bullies. What do you say to that?"

Daviel looked the boy straight in the eye and said, "No way!"

The boy was surprised and released his grip on Daviel's shirt. Feeling the release in pressure, Daviel jerked his arm and ran away. Just then he saw the judge drive up and ran for the car. Before entering the car, he looked around and saw Hal getting into his car.

Monday at school Daviel carefully avoided the bullies. He was able to do this until Friday, when the teacher sent him to the principal's office to get something. On the way back to class he saw one of the bullies coming his way. He started running down the hall and as he rounded the corner, he literally ran into the leader of the bullies.

"Well if it isn't the squirt. Got my money?" he asked.

Daviel tried to get away but the bigger boy had too strong of a hold on the front of his shirt. The bully lifted Daviel off the ground and slammed him against the wall. "I said squirt, got my money?"

"No!" squeaked Daviel.

"That's too bad squirt. Guess I'll have to get rough with ya." He then pulled out a switchblade knife and slowly moved it closer to Daviel's stomach. "This thing is pretty sharp. I'll just cut off a little excess fat to show you I mean business," he said with a laugh.

Daviel's eyes shinned with fear. At four feet six inches and weighing less than ninety pounds he did not have any "fat" to cut off. He was breathing heavily in anticipation of the pain. He was just about to call for help when he heard someone coming around the corner. Before he could call out, the bully threw him to the ground and quickly put his knife away.

As the teacher rounded the corner she saw the bully helping Daviel to his feet and straightening his clothes.

"Sorry little fellow," said the bully in the nicest voice he could muster while helping Daviel straighten his clothes. "I did not mean to knock you over. I didn't see you. Hope I didn't hurt you."

The teacher hurried forward. "Are you okay?" she asked.

'I'm fine," replied Daviel. "I better go to class."

As Daviel hurried away he heard the teacher say, "You're such a good boy Leroy. Too bad all of our older boys are not as considerate as you are. You are a fine example to our younger students!"

"Thank you, ma'am," said Leroy. "I try my best. I better get back to class. Have a good day," he said with a wave as he left the teacher.

She stood there smiling to herself as she thought about Leroy and his kindness to the younger boy. What a fine example he was for the other students.

Daviel could not believe his ears. Surely, he did not hear the teacher right. That boy, Leroy, was going to cut him up and she thinks he is a good boy. He was amazed. Quickly he tucked in his shirt and hurried to class. He did not want to meet any of the other bullies.

"Only one more class," thought Daviel, "and then I can go home. As he and Hal were changing their clothes for P.E. he told Hal what had happened.

"What are you going to do?" asked Hal. "What are we going to do?"

"I do not know, but I do know this, I am not paying those bullies five dollars for their protection," he said with a determined look on his face.

After class coach called a meeting. All the boys gathered around to hear what he had to say.

"I realize," he began, "that this is the last class for the day but that does not excuse you from taking showers after class."

Daviel and Hal looked at each other and inwardly groaned. They knew what was coming next.

"I have been told that some of you boys smell when you get on the bus, therefore; you will be taking showers after class from now on. Do I make myself clear?"

"Yes sir!" chorused the boys.

On the way home Daviel was unusually quiet.

"Is something the matter?" asked the judge.

"No sir," said Daviel.

As Daviel entered the door to his house the phone started ringing.

"I got it!" he called. "Hello?"

"Is this Daviel?" asked the quiet voice.

"Yes, it is; who am I talking to?"

"It's me, Hal," said the caller. "What are we going to do?"

"About what?" asked Daviel. Daviel was very intelligent but sometimes his memory was short.

"What do you mean, 'about what'?" Hal asked. "Monday we'll have to take showers."

"Oh that," said Daviel, "I figure the coach was only talking to the boys who ride the bus home. That does not apply to us," reasoned Daviel.

"Hey, you're right. Boy am I glad. I thought my whole weekend was going to be ruined. Thanks, my friend. I'll talk to you later," said Hal before hanging up.

Daviel felt a little funny inside. Deep down inside he knew that coach was expecting everyone to take showers but he decided not to worry about it until later. The weekend passed quickly. On Monday, Daviel tried to pretend that he was sick. Mrs. McKnight, having raised four children of her own was too smart to fall for it though.

"Hmmm" she said. "You don't have a temperature. Maybe I should call the doctor. He could always give you a shot. That should —"

"A shot!" exclaimed an excited Daviel. "I feel better already. It must have been a passing thing."

After Daviel had gone to school and the judge returned home Mrs. McKnight said she needed to talk to him.

"Honey, have you noticed anything funny going on with Daviel?"

"Funny ha, ha, or funny as in STRANGE," he queried.

"Funny as in STRANGE."

Judge McKnight paused to think. "Well he has been quieter lately. I just thought maybe he was finally settling in."

"No," said Mrs. McKnight. "Something is bothering him. Something at school I think."

"I'll talk to him when he gets home today. We need to spend some time together anyhow," said the judge.

She smiled as she tried to imagine what the old man and the young boy could possibly do together. She was really fond of Daviel and very concerned about him.

Later, after Daviel had finished his homework, the judge asked him if he could help him do something.

"Yes sir," Daviel replied.

The "old man" and the "boy" went outside. They walked down the path to the judge's workshop. He opened the door and let Daviel go in first. Daviel was excited. He had never been in the judge's workshop before. His excitement disappeared when the judge said, "Want to tell me about it?"

Daviel thought fast but could not figure out what the judge meant. "About what?" he asked.

"Mrs. McKnight talked with me this morning. She seems to think that something is bothering you. She is very astute when it comes to things like this so you might as well tell me what it is, unless you would rather tell her."

"No!" said Daviel a little too quickly.

"Ah, so there is something wrong. Care to talk about it?

"No."

The judge stepped closer to the boy. He was remembering a similar conversation with one of his sons. He took Daviel in his arms and engulfed him in a hug. Daviel was shocked. Sure, the judge had patted his arm before and even playfully punched him in the arm but never this. The young boy's emotions were churning inside of him.

No one had hugged him before except his mom and dad. Deep inside he was beginning to love the judge and Mrs. McKnight and it scared him a little. He also felt a little disloyal to his parents.

Slowly Daviel relaxed and enjoyed the safety of the older man's arms. After a few minutes the judge released him and looked into his eyes.

With tears in his eyes the judge said, "I know it has been hard on you with the loss of your parents and having to come and live with strangers, especially old ones. When I first saw you in court, I saw a twelve-year-old little boy struggling to be brave and my heart went out to you. That night I talked with Mrs. McKnight and she was thrilled when I told her that I thought we should be your guardians. Both she and I have come to love you a lot. You are like our son, well maybe grandson," he said with a smile.

Daviel looked into the judge's kind face and then threw himself in his arms. He had people who loved and cared about him. He did not have to be lonely anymore. Maybe, he thought, I should tell him what is going on.

Taking a step back and with a deep breath he told the judge about the bullies and the threat. Quietly the judge listened until the boy finished his story.

The judge again looked into the boy's eyes. He believed in eye contact. "Thanks for telling me. Is there anything else bothering you?"

Daviel remained silent so the judge continued. "I remember when I was your age," he started. "Don't give me that funny look young man. I know I am old, but I can remember when I was thirteen. You're going through a lot of changes, both physically and emotionally, and I would like to help you. Do you want to talk about it?"

Daviel nodded his head and then blurted out, "The coach told us Friday that all of us have to start taking showers."

Judge McKnight stared at the boy. So that was the problem, he thought smiling to himself. He could imagine the boy's difficulty. Quietly he asked, "Have you not taken a shower for the past two weeks?"

Daviel shook his head and then said, "No sir."

"What time is your P.E. class?

"It is my last class."

"That makes it easier," said the judge. Obviously Daviel had not taken a shower today because his hair was dry when he got into the car after school. His hair was always dry. Daviel looked at him. "I have a solution: simply wait till everyone else has left then take your shower. Are you the only boy not taking a shower?"

"Oh, no sir, there are three of us. My best friend Hal hasn't taken one either and another boy. Sir, if I wait until everyone is gone then you will have to wait for me when you pick me up."

"That's okay, I do not mind. However," he said looking straight into Daviel's eyes, "I think that after the first time it will be easier the second time."

Daviel and the judge went back to the house. The judge was thinking about the bullies and what to do about them. Daviel was thinking about how nice it was to have someone who cared and with whom he could share his problems.

After a while the judge had formulated a plan and called the principal of the school, a good friend of his. He had a hard time convincing the principal about Leroy who had always been a model student. But finally, he did and the principal agreed to his plan.

Daviel learned that growing up was hard but it was a little easier after talking with someone you love and respected. From that day onward, he planned always to talk with the judge whenever he had a problem.

Monday at school, the judge had secretly arranged that Leroy and Daviel would meet again. Leroy, not knowing that the principal and the police were secretly watching the meeting, once again tormented the younger boy.

"Hello squirt, so we meet again. Where's my money."

"I told you I will never pay you protection money, so get lost."

Leroy pulled out his switchblade. Daviel stepped back. Leroy grabbed his shirt before he could run and again said he was going to slice a little fat off the boy's stomach. As he pricked Daviel's stomach with the blade drawing a little blood the principal and the police stepped out of hiding. Leroy was arrested and after investigating the matter the members of Leroy's gang were expelled from school.

Daviel talked with Hal at lunch about what had happened and about the dreaded P.E. class. At the end of the day Daviel and Hal left the gym with wet hair. A surprised judge saw the boys coming.

"Hey," he called. "I thought you were going to wait to take your showers after everyone had already left."

Daviel and Hal looked at each other and Daviel said. "We talked about it at lunch and we decided that it would not be fair to make you wait and we decided that God had made us the way we are and that He did not make mistakes. It was a little embarrassing though," he added as an afterthought.

"I am so proud of both of you!" exclaimed the judge giving the boys a big hug embarrassing them — a little. Daviel was extremely happy.

CHAPTER 3
FALSE FRIENDS

It was nearing the end of October when Daviel received an important letter. The judge called him into his study to talk to him.

Daviel wondered what he had done wrong. Since his talk with the judge in the judge's workshop he and the judge spent more time talking and doing things together but never did they talk in the judge's study.

"Sit down," said the judge. Daviel took the chair closest to him.

"Have I done something wrong?" he asked.

Smiling the judge said, "No son," then he took a large envelope from his desk drawer. "Do you know a Mr. Allerton," he asked.

Daviel thought for a minute. The name sounded vaguely familiar. He thought for a bit longer and then he remembered that his dad had mentioned his name once or twice. "I think my dad knew him."

"You are right. Mr. Allerton died and he left your dad a large sum of money and since you are your dad's heir the money now belongs to you. You are an extremely wealthy young man."

Daviel sat there quietly trying to absorb what the judge was telling him. He had turned thirteen in July with a little money to his name and now he was extremely wealthy. He wondered just how wealthy he was. "Um, Sir, how wealthy is extremely wealthy?" he asked.

The judge responded that after taxes he would be worth around fifty million dollars.

Fifty million dollars thought Daviel. Wow! The judge explained that the money would be held in trust for him but that he could draw upon the trust account whenever he needed money.

The next day they went to the bank to set up the account in both of their names. The money was Daviel's but being a minor, he needed an adult's name on the account. He needed someone he could trust and he trusted no one more than he trusted the judge.

After signing the papers Daviel was given a debit card with which he could draw out funds up to ten thousand dollars a week. Needless to say, he was very excited.

"I think it would be best Daviel if you kept your new-found wealth a secret."

"Can I tell Hal," he asked.

The judge thought about it and said, "Sure, tell Hal, but only tell him that you have come into some money but do not tell him how much."

The next day during lunch Daviel took Hal outside and told him the news. Hal could not believe his ears.

"How much money did you get?" he asked.

"The judge told me not to tell anyone."

"But I'm your best friend."

Daviel thought about it. "Okay, but you have to promise not to tell anyone. Promise?"

Hal raised his right hand and said, "I promise."

Daviel told him the amount. Hal could only stand there with his mouth open, staring at Daviel. The bell rang for classes so the two smiling boys went back into the school. Hal could not believe what he had heard. His best friend was a multi-millionaire.

Over the next few weeks Daviel and Hal planned all sorts of ways to use the money. They talked about buying an island and building a big house on it for the two of them. They talked about the cars they wanted to buy and boats and all the other things that a rich person would buy. Hal suggested that he buy a jet so that they could see the world.

At church on Sunday someone yelled "There's Daviel the millionaire."

Daviel and the judge looked at each other. How did someone find out? "Did you tell anyone?" asked the judge.

"Only Hal and he promised not to tell anyone."

"Well it looks like he told," said the judge.

Daviel jumped into the judge's car and called Hal. "You promised not to tell," he said when Hal answered.

Recognizing Daviel's voice he said, "I didn't."

"How else could they have found out? Everyone at church knows that I am a millionaire. If it was not you then who was it?"

"I promise, I told no one," Hal said. "Don't you believe me?" he asked.

"Of course, I do," said Daviel, "but the judge probably will not."

Daviel hung up the phone. Everyone crowded around him, congratulating him about his new-found wealth.

On Monday, all the kids at school knew Daviel was a millionaire. Daviel liked all the attention, however; he was not prepared for what was to follow.

Two weeks later a couple at church approached Daviel with a sob story. They said they needed ten thousand dollars for an operation for their mother. Could he help them? Daviel told them that he could draw out ten thousand dollars a week but he had no way to go to the bank.

"I will ask the judge to take me so I can draw out the money," he told the couple.

"No!" responded the man quickly. Daviel looked at him. The man explained, "I don't want to bother the judge. We have fifteen minutes before church starts. What if I take you to the bank right now? I am sure we have enough time to draw out the money and get back for church."

"Okay, but I have to tell the judge where I am going," he said as he ran off to find the judge.

Over the next several months Daviel had many new friends. He received invitations from many church families for dinner. Always during these dinners, the subject of a "need" came up and once again Daviel was taken to the bank to withdraw money.

Daviel became very popular at school. Everyone wanted to be his friend. He was really enjoying all the attention. Through it all, Hal remained a loyal friend, never asking Daviel for money. He tried a couple of times to talk to Daviel about his new "friends" but failed to get through. Daviel was having too good of a time. Hal increased his prayers for him

After six months, and two hundred thousand dollars later the judge called Daviel into his study. Daviel entered the study beaming and with a swagger in his step that he never had before.

"What can I do for you," asked Daviel.

"I think that we need to talk."

"About what?" asked Daviel.

"Sit down," began the judge. "I can tell you have enjoyed all this attention. Do you have any idea about how much money you have given away so far?" he asked.

Daviel shook his head no.

"I thought not. You have given away two hundred thousand dollars in the last six months."

"Wow!" exclaimed Daviel. He knew he had given away a lot of money but he had no idea it was that much. "Are, are you mad at me?"

"Mad, no," said the judge, "but I think we need to talk. Okay?"

"Yes sir."

"Let me ask you a question. Do you really believe that all those people who want money from you are your friends?

"I, I guess so."

"Let me ask you another question. Has Hal ever asked you for money?

"No sir."

"Who do you think is your real friend, Hal or the others?

"Hal has always been my best friend," responded Daviel with a big smile.

"Exactly, now listen to me and do not interrupt, okay?"

Daviel knew that something was wrong but still he could not figure out what it was. "Sure," he said.

The judge then explained that his real friends would not ask for money. They would accept and love him for himself and not for his money. "I have allowed you to give away money freely so that I could teach you a valuable lesson. You see, I knew this would happen though I am disappointed with the church members. I would have thought they would have acted better. Greed is a terrible sin. This is what I want us to agree about. Do you trust me?"

"Of course," said Daviel

"Would you give me your debit card if I asked you to?"

Quickly Daviel took out his debit card and gave it to the judge.

"Daviel, you are like a son to me. Those so-called friends are not really your friends."

"They are not?" Asked Daviel.

"No son, they're not. They are pretending to be your friend so that they can get money from you. I think I can prove that to you," said the judge.

"How?" asked Daviel

"I want you to understand that having a lot of money means being responsible enough to use it wisely. Here is my plan. The next time anyone asks you for money you tell them that you can no longer take money out of your account because I took away your card. Now all withdrawals have to go through me. Okay?"

"Yes sir, but how will that prove who is my friend and who is using me?" Daviel asked.

"Your real friends, like Hal, will not care, but those who only want you for your money will soon learn that you cannot give them any more and I am afraid they will not stay around. I do not wish to hurt you but I do not want them to rob you blind. Will you agree to my plan?"

Daviel thought for a moment. "Yes sir. What if they do not leave, will I get my card back?"

The judge thought for a moment. He knew the friends would leave but that they would come back when he had his card back. Finally, he said, "I will give you your card back only if we spend time talking about how to handle money correctly. Do we have a deal?"

Smiling Daviel said, "Deal."

Soon word got out that the well had run dry. Within a couple of weeks all the "new friends" disappeared. The judge did not say anything to Daviel but waited for Daviel to come to him.

One night after church Daviel asked the judge if they could talk. They had been meeting frequently to discuss finances so the judge knew it was about something else.

"How about when we get home?" he asked.

"Thanks," was all Daviel said.

That night the judge was in his study when there was a knock at the door. "Come in."

Daviel entered and said before even sitting down, "You were right."

The judge went to the boy and hugged him. "You have learned a very valuable lesson. As long as you have money you will always be a target for false friends. A lot of older men have lost their fortunes to so called friends."

"I am glad I had you," said Daviel.

Before the judge could respond there was another knock at the door. "May I come in?" asked Mrs. McKnight.

"Sure," Daviel said.

The three of them discussed the situation together.

"There is one more thing that we need to discuss. Being rich is a temptation not to depend on the Lord for your needs; after all, you can buy whatever you want. However, Daviel, it is very important that you continue having your devotions and prayer time each day with the Lord. Ask him daily what he would have you do, especially with all your money. Seek His advice daily and daily live for Him. Remember, it is a great temptation to trust in yourself and your money, but son, you must depend on the Lord. He can always cause you to be poor again. Remember, your happiness in life does not come from being rich but from being a child of God and following Him with your whole heart."

"Yes sir, I will remember that but maybe you and mom could remind me from time to time?"

After an hour of talking the judge offered to give Daviel his card back. "Thank you," Daviel said. "I do not want it. I was wondering if maybe I could have an allowance each week. That would give me some money but not too much. I would like to be able to buy things for Hal and myself from time to time."

"Hal is a really good friend. His kind is very rare. You want to hang on to him," explained Mrs. McKnight.

Daviel's face lit up. "You know, with friends like you and Hal, I really do not need any more."

"That young man," said the judge "is the best lesson that you have learned so far. Oh yeah, in my devotions this morning I found a verse for you: Proverbs 19:6

"Many will entreat the favor of the prince: and every man is a friend to him that giveth gifts."

"Wow! That sounds like me. While I was giving away gifts of money I had many friends but when the money stopped all my "friends" left. I still believe Hal. I know he did not tell anyone about my being rich," said Daviel

"You're right," said the judge. "I found out yesterday what happened."

"Well, don't keep us in suspense!" Mrs. McKnight exclaimed.

"It seems that when we left the bank one of the church members saw us leave. When he entered the bank, he heard the employees talking about a boy and his new-found wealth. He asked the teller who they were talking about. The teller said that he could not give any names but that the boy who had just left is now a millionaire. Our "friend" put two and two together. I need to apologize to Hal for not believing him."

"Who was the church member?" asked Mrs. McKnight.

"That my dear is a secret," he said and they all laughed.

"I have one more question," said Daviel. "The Bible says that I need to tithe on my money. That would be five million dollars. Do I write a check to the church or what?"

"That is a very good question Daviel," said the judge. "You are right. God does expect you to tithe and five million dollars would be the correct amount."

"That is a lot of money," said Mrs. McKnight. "I wonder what the church will do with all that money."

"That, my dear, is not our problem, thankfully. Daviel, you need to write a check to the church and put it in the offering plate. Everyone will know that it came from you but that cannot be helped. It is always best to obey the Lord."

"If I write a check for five million dollars then everyone will know that I inherited fifty-million-dollars, right?"

"That is true. You could write a check for one million this week and then a little later write another one until you have given the five million," said Mrs. McKnight

"No, I think it would be best to just write one check. Who cares if everyone knows how much I inherited. It is God's money anyway," declared Daviel.

"That is correct. It is God's money. I am very proud of you son!" said the judge.

Back in the Taxi….

CHAPTER 4

A True Need

During the taxi ride home Daviel wondered what he could do to help Drew and his grandmother. Surely there was something he could do. He would talk to the judge about it.

When Daviel got home he found a note saying that the judge and Mrs. McKnight were going out for the evening and that they would be very late getting home. There was a plate of food in the fridge that he could microwave and ice cream in the freezer for a snack.

Daviel ate his food in silence. After washing his plate and silverware the phone rang. Looking at the caller ID he saw that it was his best friend.

"What is up?" asked Daviel.

"Nothing!" said Hal. "I was wondering if you found Drew's house."

Daviel told his friend the whole story. Hal laughed so much that his sides hurt.

"What was the grandmother's name," he asked Daviel.

"Leti, why?"

Laughing Hal said, "What kind of name is that. I've never heard of anyone called Leti."

"After she calmed down and realized who I was she was really nice. I want to do something to help her and Drew but I do not know what to do. I plan to ask the judge about it. Do you have any suggestions?"

The boys talked for a while, and then hung up. Daviel fixed himself some ice cream and ate it while watching a movie. After washing up he went to bed. Daviel awoke early the next morning. He was anxious to ask the judge what he could do to help Drew and his grandmother. He made himself some cereal for breakfast. While eating, Mrs. McKnight came into the kitchen.

"My, you're up early this morning. What time did you go to bed?" she asked.

"I went to bed around eleven," replied Daviel. "I had some ice cream while I watched a movie and then went to bed. What time did you get in?"

"We got home about midnight."

"Did you have a good time?" asked Daviel politely. What he really wanted to know was: when would the judge get up.

"Oh, my, yes!" exclaimed Mrs. McKnight. "The ballet was magnificent. You should go see it!"

"Uh, no thanks," stammered Daviel. The last thing he wanted to do was go to the ballet! "I am glad you enjoyed it though," he said as Mrs. McKnight smiled and ruffled his hair.

The first few times she had done that Daviel did not like it but now he kind of enjoyed it. He realized that whenever she ruffled his hair she was saying 'I love you' only without words. It made him feel good inside.

"Mom, when will dad be waking up?" he asked.

"The judge left hours ago. He had an important meeting at six this morning. How that man can continue to go with so little sleep is beyond me — and at his age!"

She saw the disappointed look on Daviel's face and asked, "Is something wrong?"

"No, nothing is wrong. I just wanted to get his advice about something."

"Can I help?" she asked.

Daviel told her about his episode with Leti, Drew's grandmother. Mrs. McKnight laughed at the funny way that he told the story.

"My, my, you did have a time, didn't you? I'm glad that it all worked out okay. What's the problem," she asked kindly.

"Well, they live in a really bad section of town. I like Drew and, well, I think that growing up in that area of town would not be good for him. I want to help them but I do not know what to do." He looked at his "mom" for some advice.

"You do have a problem. I know your heart is in the right place but it would be hard to help them when they haven't asked for it. You don't want to offend them." She stopped talking to think about the situation.

"I have an idea. Why don't you invite Drew and Leti over for lunch on Saturday? That way dad and I could get to know them and maybe after that we could formulate a plan. How old is Drew?"

"He is thirteen."

"Oh, so he's almost your age," she said. "For some reason I thought he was younger."

"Actually," stated Daviel, "he just turned thirteen and I will be fifteen next month."

Smiling, Mrs. McKnight said, "I see, that does make a difference."

Daviel looked at her face to see if she was teasing him. She was. "Is he a Christian," she asked.

"I do not know. I did not think to ask. I thought that maybe Hal could go with me to visit him when I go next time."

"That would be good. When do you plan to go?" she asked.

Daviel was staring into space deep in thought and did not hear the question.

Mrs. McKnight cleared her throat and asked again, "When do you plan to go?"

"I am sorry! I was thinking. I paid his bill at the hospital. Do you think that was okay?" He asked timidly.

Mrs. McKnight, or mom, gave him a giant hug. "You are a wonderful young man. I am sure they will appreciate your kindness."

"They will not know that I paid it. I told them to keep that a secret. Later this week they will receive a letter telling them that someone paid the bill for them. They do not have to know it was me. Can I call them and invite them to dinner?"

"Certainly, and tell them that you and the judge will pick them up and take them back home. Maybe Hal could go with you," she said as an afterthought.

Daviel ran to the phone to talk with Hal. After asking his parents for permission Hal said he could go with him the next time he visited Drew. "Ask your parents if you can spend the night on Friday," suggested Daviel.

"Have the judge and Mrs. McKnight said it was okay?"

"I have not asked them but you know they will not mind." Hal groaned into the phone. "Wait and I will ask," said Daviel.

Daviel put down the phone and asked his mom. Readily she gave her permission. "Mom said it would be fine and for you to come for dinner." Daviel waited while Hal asked his parents.

"What time should dad bring me over," asked Hal.

"Come as early as you can. Mom just said 'why don't you spend the weekend with us?' We will bring you to church on Sunday."

Daviel held the line while Hal asked his parents. "Great!" exclaimed Daviel when Hal said he could stay the whole weekend. "Be here by two o'clock," said Daviel and then he hung up the phone.

Daviel called Drew and asked if he and his grandmother could come to lunch on Saturday. Drew checked with his grandmother and plans were made. They would pick them up at eleven-thirty.

The judge or dad came home late that evening. He went to Daviel's room.

"Mom said you needed some advice?"

"Yes sir," responded Daviel sitting up in his bed. The judge sat beside him ready to listen. Daviel told him the story about Leti and the hat. The judge smiled and waited for Daviel to continue.

"Dad, I have been thinking and praying about what God would have me to do with all my money. I believe that He gave it to me so that I could help others but I do not know how to go about doing that. I want to help Drew and his grandmother but I do not know what to do."

The judge could hear the frustration in the boy's voice. He was really proud of this young man. Embracing Daviel in a giant bear hug he told Daviel how proud he was of him. Then he said, "Why don't we wait until Saturday. Maybe they will say something that will help you decide what to do. I hear Hal is spending the weekend with us. That will be fun."

Daviel looked at his dad to see if he was being sarcastic. He knew the judge really liked Hal but they sometimes got a little noisy when they were together.

"By the way, what happened to Drew?" asked the judge.

"You know the driver of the car did not stop after hitting Drew, right?" The judge nodded his head. Daviel continued, "Drew has some badly bruised ribs and two broken wrists. I guess it could have been a lot worse. I am glad I was there to help him."

"Mom said that Drew is about your age, correct?"

Mrs. McKnight had told the judge the whole story including Daviel's emphasis that Drew only just turned thirteen and that he was almost fifteen.

"Yes sir," was all that Daviel said.

"Why don't we wait and see what Saturday brings," suggested the judge. "What time is Hal coming tomorrow?"

Daviel told him at two.

Hal arrived the next day promptly at two. Daviel met him at the driveway and the two carried his bag to Daviel's room running up the stairs.

"I heard the new amusement park opened today," said the judge when the boys came back downstairs. "How would you like to go check it out?"

"Really!" shrieked the two boys.

Mrs. McKnight came running in to see what all the noise was about. After hearing the explanation, she said that it would be awfully crowded. The boys did not seem to mind. The judge drove them to the park and dropped them off. It was decided that the judge would return for them at ten. After making sure they had plenty of money he said goodbye.

After waiting in line for long periods of time to ride a few rides the boys decided to leave and come back another day. They could take a taxi home so they would not have to bother the judge. Daviel bought them both season passes so that they could visit the park whenever they wanted. On the way to the front gates Daviel grabbed Hal's arm.

"Hal, see that man over there?" he asked pointing to a man about thirty-five years old. "He looks like the driver of the car that hit Drew."

"Which man?" asked Hal. There were several men standing around.

"The tall one in the grey pullover and blue pants," explained Daviel.

Hal looked at the man but could not see the man's face. The man was tall and thin and had very big ears.

"How do you know he's the man?" asked Hal.

"I am not sure, but with that nose and those ears he looks like the man I saw driving away from the accident. I did not actually see him hit Drew," explained Daviel, "but a car came around the corner from the right direction. There were not any other cars in sight and the car was red. Drew said that the car that hit him was red with a black stripe down the side. Let's follow him. If he has a red car with a black stripe then it may be him"

The boys followed the man for two hours. Since the park was so crowded they had no problem staying out of sight. It was getting close to ten o'clock. They decided to call the judge to explain that they may be a little late. The judge listened to Daviel and told him to be careful. While they were talking the man headed for the exit.

"Dad, the man is leaving. We will follow him to his car. Maybe we can get his license plate number. I will call you back," explained Daviel as he hung up.

They followed him out of the park and into the parking lot. There were fewer people out here so they had to be more careful not to be seen. The man was heading for the far side of the lot so the boys, instead of following the man down the row he had taken, turned down the preceding row and followed. They could see a red sports car at the end of the row the man had taken but did it have a black stripe down the side?

When the boys were halfway down their row a man entered from another row and started following them. Because they were so absorbed in watching the man they did not realize it. They were being shadowed!

They saw the man get into the sports car. Quickly they hurried to the end of the row. Would they be able to get the tag number? As they got close to the end of their row they heard the sports car start and then someone grabbed them from behind turning them around.

When they were grabbed the boys let out a low gasp. "What's going on here?" asked a security guard.

They did not have time to explain. The man in the red car was getting away. Hal turned and saw that the car had a black stripe down the side.

Excitedly he said, "Daviel, it has a black stripe."

"Could you see the license plate number?" asked Daviel while trying to look.

Before Hal could answer the guard said, "All right, I'll ask you one more time. What's going on here?"

"We think that man is a hit and run driver," explained Daviel. "We were following him to his car so that we could get his license plate number."

Daviel looked downhearted. Then his face lit up. "Could you call the front gate and ask them to write down the tag number for us. It is very important. PLEASE?" asked Daviel.

The guard hesitated but called on his walkie-talkie and made the request. "Come with me," he said.

The guard took the boys to the front gate and asked if they were able to get the tag number. They were told that the car had left as they got the call. They did not have time to get the number.

Hal looked dejected but Daviel said, "Cheer up! At least we know that he lives in the area. Maybe we will see him again."

"Uh hum," said the guard. "I believe you boys have some explaining to do."

"Yes sir," chorused the boys.

They told the guard their story. As he was trying to make up his mind whether to believe the boys or not the judge drove up. Getting out of his car and seeing the boys with the security guard he asked, "Is there a problem sir?"

"Dad!" exclaimed Daviel.

Upon seeing the famous judge, the guard started to stammer, "Y-You know these boys."

"Yes sir, Daviel is my son and Hal is his best friend. Do you mind telling me what they have done?"

The guard explained what had happened and why he had apprehended the boys. "I meant no harm, sir," said the guard.

"No problem son, you were just doing your job." Then turning to the boys, he said, "Too bad you didn't get the tag number."

They got in the car and went home. The next morning, they picked up Leti and Drew. Drew had to be fed his dinner because he could not hold a fork. Daviel and Hal had a fun time feeding him. After dinner they sat around talking.

"Judge McKnight, sir, do you think you could help me?" asked Leti.

"What seems to be the problem?" he asked.

"My grandson cannot take a bath or shower by himself. Obviously, he cannot hold the soap and he cannot get the casts wet, but he won't let me bathe him," Leti explained.

Drew's face turned bright red. Daviel and Hal laughed.

"I take it young man that you have not had a bath for a few days," said the judge.

Blushing Drew said, "No sir."

"Dad," cut in Daviel. "Hal and I could give him a bath."

"What about it?" asked the judge looking at Drew.

Still blushing, the boy said that he guessed that would be okay.

The boys headed upstairs to Daviel's bedroom. "Do you want a bath or shower?" asked Hal.

"I can't get the casts wet so I guess it'll have to be a bath," Drew explained.

Hal started the bath water and Daviel helped Drew get undressed. Thirty minutes later a clean and nice-looking boy came down the stairs.

"Now that looks much better!" exclaimed Leti. Turning to the boys she asked, "How about you boys coming to the house twice a week and giving Drew a bath. That surely would be a big help to me, if it won't be too big of a problem for you," she added quickly. "I could pay you a little something for your trouble."

Daviel looked at his parents then said, "I could take a taxi to your house and you will not have to pay me anything. I will be glad to help." Looking at his parents he asked, "What do you think?"

Before they could answer Hal asked, "What about me?"

"I would come and get you in the taxi and then we would go together."

The judge said that it would be fine with him. "Didn't you tell your mom that you wanted to visit Drew? Now you can see him twice a week. Would that be okay with you Drew?"

"YES SIR!" said Drew. "Um, you know that we do not live in the best section of town, right."

Smiling the judge said, "Your grandmother and I were discussing that problem. I think we have a solution."

"That's great!" exclaimed the boy. "What is it?"

"There is a modest but well kept up house over by our church. Leti told me that you and she always attended church until you had to move." Drew nodded his head yes. "The house is empty and I think we could move you both into it in the next few days."

Drew's face fell.

"What's wrong?" asked the judge.

"We, we couldn't afford to buy a nice place nor could we pay the rent on one. Grandma only has her social security check and a small pension from grandpa and I'm too young to get a job," replied Drew.

Daviel started to say something but the judge stopped him. "That's not a problem. I happen to know someone who recently asked me if I knew of a family that he could help out."

"But sir," interrupted Drew. "Grandma doesn't take charity."

Smiling the judge continued, "This isn't charity. He told me that the Lord had blessed him with a lot of money, he's a multi-millionaire, and he felt that he should use it to help others. You wouldn't be accepting charity but a gift of love from the Lord Himself and you would be giving my friend a blessing."

Drew's eyes lit up and then he looked at his grandmother. "Would that be okay?"

"I already told the judge we would love to move into the house. You would be able to go to a better school. In fact, the judge said you could go to the Christian School with Daviel and Hal. I, I can't give you all the things I would like, and Drew, this would be a blessing to us both."

Smiling from ear to ear Drew asked, "How soon can we move?"

Everyone laughed.

"Hey, I just remembered something. Drew, remember the car that hit you."

"Yes."

"You said it was a red car with a black stripe down the side. Can you remember anything else about it?" coaxed Daviel.

"It was a small sports car. It had only two doors. Oh, yeah, I remember something else. The man inside, you know, the one with the big nose and ears, he must be pretty tall because I remember wondering how he could fit inside such a small car."

"We saw him or at least we think we did!" exclaimed Daviel.

Everyone was excited as they discussed what they should do next. After talking for a while they took Leti and Drew back home.

The next week Leti and Drew moved into their new home. The "friend" bought them the house, new clothes, and paid the tuition for Drew's school. From time to time as they had needs a money order would come in the mail. Drew asked Daviel how the man could know their needs and Daviel simply answered 'God'.

CHAPTER 5
FALSE LEADS

Daviel, the judge and Mrs. McKnight continued to look out for needs that Daviel could use his money on. All of them: Daviel, Hal, Drew, Mrs. McKnight, the judge and Leti kept a sharp eye out for the man in the small red sports car.

Since the new house was close enough for the boys to ride their bikes, Daviel and Hal went to Drew's house every day to help him get dressed and twice a week to give him his bath. The three boys were becoming good friends.

"Drew, Drew," called his grandmother.

"Coming," yelled Drew. He and his two friends went into the kitchen to see what his grandmother needed.

"Could you three boys mosey on down to the corner grocery store and buy the things on my list?" asked Drew's grandmother.

"Be glad to," said Daviel taking the list and money. "Come on boys. We can look out for you know who on the way."

It was hard for Drew with his wrists in casts. He couldn't do a lot. Whenever the three boys were outside or if they went somewhere they kept a sharp lookout for the tall thin man with the big ears and big nose.

The boys got to the store without seeing any suspicious characters. They had put almost everything on the list into their shopping cart and Daviel said, "All we have left is the frozen food items."

Daviel was interrupted when Drew tapped him on the shoulder.

"Look!" he said pointing to a man looking at some fruit. "He could be the man that hit me."

"He does have big ears but I think he would be a taller man. Hal, walk past him and look at some apples. When you come back look and see if he has a big nose," ordered Daviel.

"You got it," responded Hal. He went to the apple bin, looked at some apples and then returned. He looked at the man's face and sure enough he had a big nose. Hal was excited as he walked back to his friends.

"Hey guys, he has a whopper of a nose!" reported Hal.

"Is he the man?" asked Drew.

"I do not know," said Hal.

"But you followed him at the amusement park," said Drew.

"We did," Daviel said, "but Hal never really saw his face, only a profile. Here is the plan. We do not have anything that will spoil or thaw in the cart so let us go and check the parking lot for a red sports car with a black stripe."

The boys agreed to Daviel's plan. They went to the parking lot, separated, and looked for a small red sports car with a black stripe. They met at the end of the parking lot. Each boy reported, "No red car,"

Disappointed they started towards the store's entrance.

"I have an idea," said Hal. "Why don't you two go in and get the rest of grandma's groceries while I run to the back of the store to look for the red car. You can follow the man until you can get a look at his face. That way we will be sure he is or is not the right man."

"Good plan," said Drew.

The boys split up. Daviel and Drew retrieved the shopping cart and proceeded to the frozen food section. Hal ran around to the back of the store.

While the two boys were getting the items on the list Hal was having his own problems.

"Here comes our man," said Drew. "You can see him in the mirror."

Daviel looked in the mirror and sure enough he could plainly see the man's face. He was not the man that he had seen driving away from the scene of the accident.

"He is not the right man," whispered Daviel to Drew.

"You're right, but he sure does have big ears and a big nose. It is a whopper!" exclaimed Drew with a laugh.

They went to the checkout line, paid for the groceries, and then went outside to meet Hal; but he was nowhere to be seen. They waited for five minutes. During this time the "suspect" left the store and got into a large green car and drove away.

The boys laughed at themselves. "At least we had a little excitement," said Drew.

Daviel smiled at the younger boy. He was getting concerned about Hal.

"Drew, stay with the cart while I go look for Hal. He should have been back long ago."

Daviel ran to the back of the store. At the far end he saw a red sports car. With his heart pounding with excitement he started running. When he was almost there he slowed down. Maybe, he thought, Hal had seen the car and he was captured when he ran to it. Slowly Daviel walked so as not to draw attention. As he got closer to the red car he heard an angry man yelling.

"All right, punk, I will give you one more chance to explain what you were doing to my car!" shouted the man.

Daviel passed the red car and saw a man holding Hal off the ground by the front of his shirt. Hal looked so funny that he would have laughed if the situation was not so serious.

"I, I," squeaked Hal. "I wasn't doing anything to your car, sir. I was just looking at it."

"Sure, you were," said the man. "I'm going to call the cops."

"Wait!" yelled Daviel as he ran up to the man holding Hal.

"Who are you?" asked the angry man. "Are you part of his gang?"

"Gang?" asked Daviel. "No sir, my name is Daviel. I am Judge McKnight's son. Please let me explain."

After hearing that Daviel was Judge McKnight's son he set Hal back on the ground. "Okay," he said, "but be quick about it."

Daviel told him the whole story as fast as he could. The man apologized and explained that there had been a lot of car vandalism at the store. He again apologized and the boys said that they understood. The man went back into the store and the boys joined Drew. On the way home, they both told their sides of the story.

Drew told about the man not being the right one. Hal explained about seeing the red sports car and running to it. It did not have a black stripe but he thought he should check it out anyway. When he got close to the car he set off the alarm. As he was getting ready to run a man came out and grabbed him. They knew the rest.

The boys were later getting home than they should have been and grandma (all three boys called her grandma) was getting worried.

"Well, it's about time ya got home. I was pert near outta my mind with worry." Grandma always reverted back to her country way of talking when she was excited.

"Sorry," said the boys. As Drew explained what had happened they helped grandma put away the groceries.

"These things weren't on the list!" exclaimed Grandma looking at Daviel.

"Oh, I, um, put a few extra things into the cart. I paid for them with my allowance money," he quickly explained giving grandma her change.

Up in Drew's room the boys talked.

"I sure thought we had found our man," said Drew.

For a while they talked about the man and where they might find him.

Daviel and Hal needed to get back home. During the next few days the three boys kept a lookout for the tall man with the big ears and big nose.

At dinner one night the Judge said, "I think I may have a lead for you."

Hal and Daviel looked at the Judge expectantly. Hal was spending the weekend with Daviel.

The judge continued, "Yesterday, while I was downtown, I saw a man going around a corner. He had big ears and was tall and slim. I tried to catch up with him but he disappeared into one of the buildings."

"Could we go downtown tomorrow to look?" asked Hal.

"You could, but tomorrow is Saturday and if the man works downtown I doubt that he would be there. However," continued the judge, "what if I take you boys downtown on Monday. You could look in the stores for possible birthday presents. You both have a birthday in a couple of weeks. You could keep a look out for the man at the same time."

The boys could not wait until Monday. Saturday morning, they rode their bikes to Drew's house. They told him about the plan. He too was excited and wished that he could go but he had a doctor's appointment to check his wrists. The boys promised to let him know what they found out, if anything.

Monday morning was bright and sunny. At breakfast the judge asked if the boys were ready for a big day. He took the boys downtown and showed them where he had seen the suspect. He told the boys that he would come back for them around five.

"That will not be necessary," said Daviel. "We can take a taxi home."

Agreeing to the plan the judge dropped the boys at the corner.

Downtown consisted of several blocks with little stores and some bigger stores. At one end of town there were stores like Sears, J.C. Penney, and Target. The other stores were the type you would find in any small town downtown shopping area. There was the local hardware store, shoe stores, book stores, second hand stores, and everything that you could imagine in between.

The boys first walked around the different blocks to look for the red car. They did not find it, but they were not discouraged because there were many places the car could be parked that they could not see. They had a wonderful time looking in the different stores for birthday presents. They found several things that they liked and wrote them down in a small notebook that Daviel always carried with him. He liked being a detective. They ate lunch at one of the local chicken restaurants that was famous for its broasted chicken.

After lunch they went to the center of town. There was a gazebo and they sat on the steps eating their ice cream cones. Hal spotted him first. He hit Daviel and pointed at a tall, thin man with large ears.

"Come on!" exclaimed Daviel as he got up to follow the man.

The boys followed him into the hardware store. A salesman asked them what they were looking for. Hal made up something and the salesman took them to the back of the store. By the time they could leave, without buying anything, the suspect was gone.

About a half hour later they spotted the man entering Sears. They were several blocks away so they ran to catch up. As they entered the store they saw him going up the escalators. He was getting off as they were getting on. They checked the sporting goods department, jewelry department, men's department, and the bathroom but could not find the man. While leaving the bathroom they spotted the man going down the escalators.

"One thing for sure," said Hal, "with all this running around we are getting our exercise."

Daviel agreed with him. "Hurry, we have to find him before he leaves the store."

They managed to follow the man into several more stores but they never got a chance to look at his face. After following him, into an exclusive men's clothing store, a salesclerk asked them if he could help them. He was a little snobbish and looked down on the boys who were dressed for chasing someone and not for an exclusive men's store.

"Our birthday is in a couple of weeks and my dad told us to look around for things that we might want. I could use a new suit for church. Mine is getting a little small," explained Daviel.

The clerk looked skeptical but led Daviel to a fitting room to be measured.

"Maybe you should wait out here," said Daviel to Hal with a wink.

"Sure." said Hal. He walked over to look at some ties while keeping his eye on the front door. A sales clerk asked him if he could help him with anything. Hal said that he was waiting for his friend who was being fitted.

Thirty minutes later Daviel had the information for his dad so he could order a suit. Daviel did find one that he really liked and hoped his dad would get it for him. If not, he would buy it himself.

"Did the man leave?" he asked Hal.

"I haven't seen him and I have kept my eyes on the door," explained Hal. "Maybe there is another door."

Daviel asked the sales clerk about the man with the big ears. He was told that the man left a while ago out the back door as it was closer to where he worked.

Disappointed, the boys left. They decided to go to the corner where the judge had seen the man. They looked in several of the store windows, window shopping.

Hal grabbed Daviel's arm. He had spotted the man in the window. They turned around in time to see the man go around the corner.

"Hurry!" exclaimed Daviel.

The boys ran around the corner right into the man they had followed all day.

"Whoa boys, where's the fire?" asked the man with a twinkle in his eyes.

"Sorry sir," said Hal looking at the man.

Daviel said, "We thought you were someone else and we were running to catch up with you. We are sorry for running into you."

"That's all right," said the man. "Sorry I am not who you thought I was." He chuckled as he watched the boys walk down the sidewalk. "Youth, oh to have that much energy again," thought the man.

When Daviel and Hal turned the corner, they broke out into fits of laughter.

Laughingly Hal said, "Just think, we have been shadowing that man for hours and he doesn't have a big nose."

Daviel was laughing so hard that his sides were hurting. "I guess we might as well go home," he said and hailed a taxi.

"How did the investigating go?" asked the judge as they entered the house.

Mrs. McKnight entered and the boys told them about their day. She and the judge laughed at all the time spent trying to see the face of the "suspect."

A whole week passed with nothing exciting happening. Daviel and Hal were spending the weekend at Drew's house. They were talking about the case and how discouraged they were getting.

Daviel had been quiet for a while. Finally, he said, "I have a plan." Drew and Hal stopped talking and looked at him.

"I think we should go to the park where Drew was hit by the car. Maybe, if we hang out there we will spot the car. Maybe he lives near there."

Saturday morning grandma packed them a lunch and the boys took a taxi to the park. It was too far away to ride their bikes and that would have been difficult for Drew anyway with his broken wrists. They made arrangements with the taxi driver to come back for them around four o'clock.

The boys played in the park and kept a sharp look out for the car. At noon they ate their lunch, still looking for the car. After lunch Daviel and Hal played Frisbee golf while Drew watched. Daviel chose the first hole. They had to throw their Frisbee across the grassy lawn and hit the trash can on the far side. Daviel won in three throws compared to four throws for Hal. Hal said that they had to land on the bench of the farthest picnic table. Again, Daviel won in four throws compared to Hal's five throws. Daviel was winning by two. Next Daviel chose a target that was far away. At the far end of the grassy area was a stone statue. They had to hit the base of it. After throwing their first two throws Daviel realized his mistake. Hal could throw farther than he could. The only thing that might help him to win this round was that he could throw straighter than Hal. Where Hal's throws went further they also had a tendency to curve.

Hal was encouraged. "Hey little brother!" he called to Daviel who was about ten feet behind him, "It looks like this is where I catch up!"

"Not in this lifetime big brother," responded Daviel and he threw with all his might.

Daviel's Frisbee did go farther but it curved. He learned that throwing with a little less power might make his Frisbee not go as far as Hal's but it did go straight and he felt that ultimately that would be to his advantage.

Hal won that round by two. They were now even.

"See that tree with the fork in it," said Hal while pointing to a dogwood tree with a large fork or branch in it. "You have to throw the Frisbee between the fork and then land in the trashcan beside it."

Hal threw first and made it halfway to the tree. Daviel threw his Frisbee in a straight line and made it a little farther than Hal's.

They ran to their Frisbees and picked them up. "I am beating you brother!" exclaimed Daviel.

"Not for long," Hal responded.

Hal's second shot hit the right branch of the fork and fell to the ground.

"Good try!" shouted Daviel, "now watch an expert."

Because he could throw straight he was fairly confident that he would make it between the two branches. Throwing his Frisbee, he watched it sail between the two branches and land not more than five feet from the trash can."

"Lucky throw," called Hal. He knew that if he threw his Frisbee just right and with a little luck he could sink it in the trash can. He took a deep breath and threw the Frisbee. Again, it hit the right branch of the fork.

"Better luck next time," Daviel said. Easily he threw his Frisbee into the trash can.

The boys played Frisbee golf for several hours. Hal called for long shots which were to his advantage and Daviel called for trick shots which he was better at.

Daviel managed to win the game by two points. Drew congratulated the boys on a good game and promised them that when his wrists were healed he would beat them both. At four the taxi driver returned.

"That was a wasted day," said Drew.

"I do not know," said Daviel. "We had fun together at the park."

"Sure, but we didn't see the car or the man," said Drew.

"There's always tomorrow," said Hal.

CHAPTER 6

THE AMUSEMENT PARK

During the summer Daviel and Hal spent a lot of time together. Today they were giving Drew his bath. Drew was protesting loudly that he was able to bathe himself.

"Of course, you can," said Daviel laughingly, "But you have two more weeks before the casts come off and until then, Hal and I have a job to do."

"That's right old boy," mimicked Hal, "we have a job to do."

The doctor said that Drew was healing nicely but that he wanted to wait a little longer before taking the casts off so that his bones would be stronger.

After his bath Drew said, "You know, it seems odd to me that we haven't been able to spot that red car. It's like it has just disappeared."

"Maybe he knows that we are looking for it and is driving another car," surmised Hal.

"I have been thinking that maybe we should go to the amusement park again," said Daviel.

"What good would that do?" asked Hal. "We have been several times and haven't seen him."

"True, but," he said turning to face Hal, "It has just occurred to me that when we saw him there it was on a Friday. We have been going on Saturday. What if he only goes on Fridays?"

"That's a good idea," Drew declared. "Tomorrow is Friday. I wish I could go with you."

"Why can you not go?" asked Daviel. "It would be a lot of fun for the three of us. We probably should find someone to go with us though. I know, how about Sherri," said Daviel pinching Hal in the stomach.

With a red face Hal said, "That would be okay with me."

The other two boys laughed. They both knew that Hal was interested in the pretty girl.

"While we are at it, maybe we could invite —"

Daviel cut Hal off. "I think we should maybe invite another boy. Any suggestions as to whom we should invite?"

The boys thought and decided to invite someone closer to Drew's age.

"I know" said Drew, "Bobby is in my Sunday school class and we have become pretty good friends. What about him? I guess we should ask grandmother if I can go first."

The boys found her in the kitchen making a snack for them. Drew asked if he could go with the boys. Looking at them with a curious expression she asked "How do you plan to ride the rides with two broken wrists?"

"Well, I, um, you know," stammered Drew.

Daviel came to his rescue. "There are a lot of rides that he could ride without hurting his wrists. He probably should not ride the roller-coasters but there are a lot of shows he could see and besides that, while we are on the rides he could be looking for the man with the big ears and nose."

They explained their theory to Leti. She thought that it sounded plausible. "If the judge thinks it is a good idea I'll let ya go."

Quickly the boys called the judge. He said he thought it was a great idea so the boys called Bobby who received permission to go with them as long as he was home by ten o'clock.

"Why don't you have Bobby spend the weekend here? He would be here for church since we live so close. Would you like that Drew?" asked Leti.

"That would be great!" exclaimed Drew. "I'll call him back right now."

It was arranged for Bobby to spend the weekend with Drew. The next morning the judge, Daviel, and Hal picked up Drew and Bobby. Daviel had anonymously bought Leti a car so that she could go to the store or the doctor's office, but she did not like to drive in really crowded areas and especially not the crowded area around an amusement park.

"Drew," said the judge. "I talked to your doctor and he said you could ride whatever rides you wanted to ride. He said your wrists were basically healed but he wants to leave the casts on for two extra weeks to be safe. He said that if your wrists start hurting to give them a rest. I would recommend that you don't ride the rides that jerk you around but all the others should be okay. Oh yeah, I forgot, the doc said no bumper cars."

"Oh man, that's one of my favorite rides," said Drew. "Why can't I ride the bumper cars?"

"Think about it. If you get hit from behind it could jar you and cause you to hit your wrists against the steering wheel and hurting them. It is better to be safe than to be sorry later," explained the judge.

"Do not worry dad, we will make sure that he obeys," said Daviel.

"How was the "spend the night" party?" asked the judge.

"It was great!" said Bobby.

The ride to the park took thirty minutes. Before dropping the boys off the judge warned them to behave and to be careful if they saw the man with the big ears and nose.

The boys promised to be careful and good. Daviel bought Drew and Bobby their season passes. Both boys thanked him. They spent the next several hours riding rides and looking for the man without success. No one had seen him.

They decided to ride the Ferris-Wheel because that would put them really high in the air and they would be able to see a lot of the park. Daviel and Hal got on first and Drew and Bobby got on several cars behind them. That way they would be looking at the ground at different times.

Bobby thought that he saw a man with big ears but when he pointed him out to Drew, Drew said, "No he has much bigger ears than that man."

A surprised Bobby said, "You must be joking. That man's ears are gigantic."

"They are big but they are small compared to our man's ears."

"He must look like Dumbo the elephant," laughed Bobby.

Back on the ground Hal asked them what was so funny. Upon hearing Bobbies comment they too laughed.

"No, his ears are not quite as big as Dumbo's, but they are huge," replied Daviel.

Next the boys rode the roller-coasters. They had some pretty high spots from which they could see a good bit of the park but no one saw him.

"Hey, what is that ride over there?" asked Bobby. "I've never seen one like that before."

"That is a free fall. It takes you high up and then drops you so that you are free falling for a little way and then they apply the brakes to slow you down. It is sort of like parachuting out of an airplane I think," explained Daviel.

"How do you know so much about it? Have you ridden it before?" asked Hal.

"No, I read about it in the newspaper. They used to be very popular in the seventies and they are trying to bring it back," Daviel said.

"It looks pretty high up. I bet we could see a lot of the park from up there especially since you get to sit for a few seconds before you drop. I think we should try it," declared Drew.

They all agreed that it would be fun. The ride was about ten stories high and you got to stay at the top for five to ten seconds before you dropped. The ride was so much fun that they rode it more than once and the best thing about it was that they could all ride together. Each time, while at the top, they looked for the man with the big nose and big ears.

Bobby spotted several men with big ears and large noses but each time he was told that their ears were too small. He could not wait to see the right man. He must have gigantic ears he thought.

It was getting late and they were getting hungry so they decided to get some lunch. The lunch court was on the other side of the park so they decided to ride the transportation cars that would take them from one side of the park to the other side. The main advantage to this was that the cars moved on rails over the heads of people walking on the ground.

"Be sure to keep a sharp lookout for our man," Daviel reminded everyone as they all boarded the large car and off, they went.

"Look at that man over there," said Drew. "He could be our man."

Daviel looked to where he was pointing. The man was eating in the food court. "When this car stops we must jump off and run to the food court. Maybe we can catch him before he leaves and follow him."

"What!" groaned Drew, "without eating lunch?"

Drew was always hungry. He said that he was a growing boy and needed to keep up his strength.

"Do you want to solve this mystery or not?" asked Hal.

Drew admitted that he did and when the car stopped they took off running. They ran to where they thought they saw the man but he was not there. They looked around for a while but never found him again.

"Guess we might as well eat," Drew said cheerfully.

Daviel and Hal laughed at their friend. "We might as well," agreed Daviel.

After lunch Hal suggested that they watch a show while their food digested.

In the dark theatre it took a while for their eyes to adjust. Daviel was looking around when he spotted the suspect.

"Hey, Drew, is that the man who hit you?" he asked.

Excitedly Drew said, "Yes, yes, it is. Come on," he said as he started walking towards the man.

"Wait!" whispered Daviel grabbing Drew's shirt. "Now is a good time to look for his car so that we can get the license plate number. It should give us about thirty minutes to search."

All three boys looked at him like he was crazy.

"What do you mean?" asked Hal.

"Well, the way I see it is, if he is watching the show then we can find his car in the parking lot before he can leave. We must get his tag number. Come on, let us get going."

Bobby was excited to finally see the man. He did have extremely large ears!

They exited the show and started towards the parking lot.

Bobby's curiosity finally got the better of him and he asked, "What's going on?"

They explained their suspicions about the man with the big ears and big nose.

"There are several big parking lots," said Hal. "Which one do we look in first?"

"I think that we should go to the same lot where we found his car the last time," explained Daviel.

"Good idea," said Drew. "Lead the way captain!"

Ignoring the remark, Daviel led the boys to the parking lot. They all got on the train that took people to their cars.

"If you see a small, red sports car holler," said Drew.

They rode around the parking lot looking for the red sports car with the black stripe. They circled the lot on the train but failed to find a red sports car.

"Let us check the next lot," said Daviel.

Getting onto another train they headed for the next lot. After riding around the lot Hal spotted a red sports car in the last row about half way down the row. The boys jumped off the train and ran to the car. It was red but did not have a black stripe.

"Well that was a waste of time," groaned Hal.

Smiling Daviel said, "The third times the charm they always say. Let us check the next lot."

They caught the next train that would take them to the station so that they could get on a different train that would take them to the next lot. They were almost finished with checking the lot when Bobby spotted a red sports car at the back of the lot under some trees. Getting off the train the boys walked to the back of the car. Daviel took out his little pad and pencil and wrote down the license plate number. He decided to call the judge with the information.

"Dad!" yelled an excited Daviel. "We found the car. Can you write down the license plate number and find out who it belongs to?"

The judge said that he would be glad to do so and that he would immediately check with the department of motor vehicles to see whose car it was. He would have the information when he picked the boys up in the evening.

CHAPTER 7

THE KIDNAPPING

The boys were excited with their success but it did not last. When they returned to the train station they were quietly put under arrest.

"If you boys will quietly come with us," said the guard. "There is no reason to make a scene." he said when Drew started to protest.

"Yes, sir, is there a problem?" asked Daviel.

"Please boys, just follow us. We will explain everything as soon as possible."

Quietly the four boys followed the man while his partner followed the boys. They led them to a building and asked the boys to please enter. Daviel realized it was the security guard house.

"Are we under arrest for something?" Daviel asked the guard.

"Let's just say you boys have some explaining to do. We saw you on our security cameras and would appreciate it if you would kindly explain what you were doing. I could understand it if you lost your car. After all, there are several large parking lots here but when you always went to little sports cars in which you all could not fit, well, would you mind explaining what you were doing, please?"

"Certainly sir," said Hal, "Daviel."

"Thanks Hal. My name is Daviel and I am Judge McKnight's son. You can call him and verify it. We —"

"We will," interrupted the guard. "Could you give us the number please?"

Daviel gave them the number but when they called it was busy.

Daviel continued with his explanation. "We were looking for a red sports car with a black stripe. My friend here was hit by one and the driver just drove off. We both got a good look at the man as he drove away and we spotted him here in the park so we decided to look for his car and get the license plate number. My dad is checking to find out who it belongs to."

"That is an interesting story. I am sure you will not mind waiting until we can contact your father," said a guard.

"Not at all, sir," responded Daviel.

"Daviel, do you remember that other guards name, you know the one who arrested us before?" asked Hal.

Upon hearing that, the head guard with raised eyebrows asked, "Do you boys make it a habit of getting arrested?"

Laughing Daviel said, "Not exactly sir. I think the other guards name was Baker, Jon Baker. He knows us."

"I am sorry boys but he is not working tonight. Try the Judge again Mike."

When the phone rang Mike gave the headset to his superior.

"With whom am I speaking please," asked the guard.

"This is Judge McKnight and to whom do I have the pleasure of speaking?" asked the judge.

"This is Officer MeGuilicuty at Six Flaggs. I currently have four boys in custody and one of them claims to be your son."

"Does he have dark red hear and green eyes and is he with a black haired boy, blond haired boy, and brown haired boy"

"Why yes he is. He said —"

Interrupting the officer, the judge asked, "And did he tell you that he was looking for a suspect in a hit and run case?"

"Why yes sir, I'm sorry sir. We obviously made a mistake but they looked suspicious. I am sorry to have bothered you and your son."

"No problem," said the judge. "May I speak to my son please?"

"Your dad wants to speak to you," said the officer handing the headset to Daviel.

"Hi dad. I am sorry about bothering you again?"

Everyone could hear the judge laughing. "No problem son; but try and stay out of any more trouble!"

"You got it dad. See you at ten."

Taking back the headset and after apologizing to the boys the officer told the boys that they were free to go.

They decided not to try and follow the "suspect" and spent the rest of the evening enjoying themselves. At ten, the judge picked up four tired boys.

On the way home, the judge said that he had the information that they wanted. "The car belongs to an Alan Mecham, the son of Senator Mecham."

"Great!" exclaimed Drew. "When can we talk to him? Alan, that is, not the Senator."

Looking at the judge's face Daviel asked, "What is wrong dad?"

"The problem is that it would be Drew's word against the senator's son's word."

"What about me?" asked Daviel.

"You did not actually see the accident," said the judge.

"That is true dad but I saw the car come from Drew's direction and there was not another car in sight, and besides that, Drew told me it was a red car with a black stripe that hit him and that is the color of the car that I saw."

"Yes son, but that is circumstantial evidence. It probably would not be enough," the judge explained.

"Does that mean we can't do anything?" asked Hal.

"No, Alan has a record as a drunk driver. There are also some rumors that he is involved in drugs. I do not know if he uses or just sells. We have an appointment to visit the Senator on Monday."

The boys were quiet for the rest of the ride home. They dropped off Drew and Bobby and after making plans to give Drew his bath on Sunday morning instead of Saturday morning, they went home.

That night Hal and Daviel lay in bed quietly talking about the case. They did not think that it was fair for Alan to get away with hitting Drew and leaving the scene of the accident.

"I bet he was drunk," said Hal. "That's probably why he didn't stop."

"Maybe," said Daviel. "I wish there was a way to get more evidence. We are not sure that Alan is the man who hit Drew. Yes, I know he fits the description and his car does too, but Drew did not really see the man too well and I only glimpsed him as he drove by."

"Maybe you will find out something when you talk to the senator," said Hal.

The boys talked about other things and finally went to sleep.

On Sunday they went to Drew's house to give him his bath. The boys helped Drew get undressed but only Daviel helped him with his bath. When they were finished Bobby took his shower. In Drew's room they helped Drew get on his Sunday clothes. Grandma, as all the boys called her, was preparing breakfast.

Bobby came into Drew's room and quickly put on his Sunday clothes. After eating breakfast, the boys carefully helped wash the dishes and after finishing them they all walked to church.

Monday morning came bright and early. The judge had Drew spend the night with Daviel so they would not have to go out of their way to pick him up.

"Good morning," said the pleasant secretary. "Do you have an appointment?" Being a temporary secretary while the real secretary was away, she did not know that the judge and the senator were good friends.

The judge told her who he was and she immediately called the senator.

"Judge McKnight is here to see you sir," she said.

She ushered them into the senator's office.

"Judge McKnight," said the senator. "To what do I owe this unexpected pleasure?"

"Good morning Senator," said the judge while shaking the senator's hand. "I know your time is valuable so I will let the boys tell you their story."

Drew and Daviel quickly told the senator their story.

"Are you sure that it was Alan who hit you, young man?" asked the Senator.

"I cannot be one hundred percent sure sir," said Drew.

"How about you, young man," the Senator asked Daviel.

"I am ninety-nine percent sure it was Alan that I saw. I want to be fair. I did not actually see the accident."

The Senator sat back in his chair and thought for a moment. "What exactly do you want from me?" he asked.

Daviel started to speak but the judge interrupted.

"We really do not want anything from you Senator Mecham. All of Drew's bills have been paid. What we really wanted to do was to let you know of the possibility that Alan was the hit and run driver. You can do what you want with the information. I just thought that you should know about it."

Senator Mecham thanked the judge for the information. He knew the judge knew about Alan's problems. "Judge, you and I are old friends. Do you think that we could talk about this privately?" he asked looking at the boys.

Daviel and Drew waited outside the office while the two men talked. Thirty minutes later Judge McKnight and the Senator came out.

"Boys," said the Senator. "I want to thank you for sharing that information with me. I promise that I will look into the matter."

With that he shook the boy's hands and went back into his office and shut the door. He looked very disturbed.

As the judge and the boys got in their car to go home Drew asked, "Sir, is that it? I mean, won't Alan have to pay for his crime."

"The Senator will sincerely look into the matter and do whatever is necessary to punish his son. However, because neither of you can be one hundred percent sure that Alan is the hit and run driver there is nothing that the law can do. A man is innocent until proven guilty."

"But dad," exclaimed Daviel. "I know that Alan is guilty."

"Are you sure enough to take an oath on the witness stand and testify against him," asked the judge.

"No sir," said Daviel dejectedly.

"I do not like it any more than you do and honestly I do not think the Senator does either. We will have to wait and see what happens after the Senator talks to his son."

Several weeks passed and no word came from the Senator about his son. Drew no longer had the casts on his wrists, for which he was very happy, and he no longer needed his friends "help".

The three friends decided that they would be on the lookout for Alan and try to see what he was doing. If they could not charge him with the hit and run accident, maybe they could find something else to charge him with. They found out where Alan lived and started watching his house. A lot of people came to and went from the house. Whenever Alan left, the boys tried to follow him. This was hard to do but one-day luck was with them.

They had been shadowing Alan as best they could for two months. This had to be done after school but they did get to follow him enough to see there was a pattern to Alan's life. Every Saturday Alan went to a park near his house. This Saturday the boys had a plan.

They would wait for Alan at the park and spy on him when he came. They saw him enter the park and head for the back fountain. The boys hid behind some shrubbery and watched as Alan took a bag out of his pocket and hid it behind a loose stone in the fountain wall.

After Alan left they would look and see what was in the bag but before they could do that another man came and removed the bag. Discouraged the boys went home.

The next Saturday the boys again waited in the park. They waited until six o'clock and finally decided to go home. Alan normally showed up in the early morning hours when there were fewer people. The boys did not know that they were being watched. The man who had retrieved the package was in hiding, spying on the boys. After seeing the boys last week, he wanted to be sure they were spying on Alan. They could have been in the right place at the wrong time the week before. Now he knew they were following Alan.

The next week Daviel borrowed the judge's high-powered camera and took pictures of Alan and the other man. Unfortunately, the boys did not know that someone else was taking pictures of them! The man had an accomplice who was taking their pictures! He would later show the pictures to Alan.

They continued to keep watch at the park but September and October passed before anything exciting happened. What had happened to Alan and the strange man?

* * *

In another part of town two men were having a discussion.

"We will not be able to use the park anymore," said the first man as he pulled out some photos. "Do you know these boys," he asked.

Alan said that he did and that the red-haired boy was the son of Judge McKnight.

"What!" exclaimed the man. "You fool! How did you ever get involved with the judge's son? Did you try to sell him drugs?"

"No, I did not try and sell him drugs. I am not that stupid. This is what happened."

Alan told the man about the hit and run and how the judge talked to his dad. When Alan finished the man was not happy.

"We're through. You will have to find another contact. Once that boy shows the judge my picture my cover will be blown if it isn't already. I am not even supposed to be in the United States. The judge will have every police officer in this state and the surrounding states looking for me. I'm out of here!"

The man stormed away leaving Alan standing there in shock. What would he do now? Alan was furious at the man and even more furious at the boys. He would find a way to make them pay.

* * *

Drew was at Daviel's house talking to him. "I think I am being followed," Drew told Daviel.

"Why would anyone want to follow you," asked Daviel.

"I don't know unless it has something to do with the hit and run accident." declared Drew.

"That was months ago," stated Daviel. "Maybe we should talk to the judge about it."

After explaining to the judge what was going on he told the boys not to worry. He thought that maybe Drew was imagining things. Daviel and Drew did not think that it was Drew's imagination and decided to tell the judge about their investigations. Daviel went to his room and got the photos that he had taken.

The judge looked at the photos and became very concerned. Now he believed Drew because the second man in the photos was a well-known drug dealer and a very dangerous man.

"I think we should notify the police," said the judge.

"About what?" asked the boys.

"You see this man," he said pointing to the photo Daviel had taken. "He is very dangerous and a known drug dealer. He is not supposed to be in this country. I think the police should watch the fountain and try to capture him and Alan."

The boys explained why that would do no good. After they had taken the pictures Alan stopped going to the park.

The judge took the photo to police headquarters and an immediate APB was put out on the man. If he was in the area the police wanted him at all costs. No expense would be spared to capture this man. They felt that if they could capture him he would lead them to bigger fish. They decided to keep an eye on Alan but were not too concerned with him at the moment. He was only small fry. They would capture him later.

Drew could not shake the feeling that he was often followed. He was beginning to be afraid to leave the house.

One day as they were playing at Drew's house the subject of Christmas came up. Drew had accepted the Lord as his savior and wanted to be baptized on Christmas day which was on a Sunday. Daviel and Hal were both excited at their friend's profession of faith. Leti said she had been saved and baptized as a young girl.

Drew was baptized by immersion on Sunday. The judge took all of them out for lunch to celebrate.

A couple of days later Drew ran into Daviel's house slamming the door and ran right into the judge. He was petrified.

The judge could tell the boy was scared especially when he felt the boy's heart beating so fast. "Calm down," said the judge, "and tell us what happened."

"My bike has a flat tire and since it is a nice sunny day and not too cold I decided to go for a walk. I really wasn't paying attention to where I was going. After a while, I started feeling like something was not right. I turned and saw a man walking behind me. He was tall—"

"Was it Alan?" Daviel interrupted.

"I don't know. He was wearing a hat pulled down low over his face with his head bent low. I could not see much of his face but the nose did look big. I don't know. Anyway, after I saw the man I started walking faster and the man picked up his pace too. I figured that he was following me. I had been walking, not really going anywhere but when I realized the man was following me I started to run. It was then that I realized that I was by that deserted stretch of woods about a mile from your house." Drew paused for breath. "I was afraid that he would kidnap me there so I ran as fast as I could and came here."

"Come on," said the judge leading the boys out the front door to his car. "Maybe we can find the man but we have to hurry."

They got into the car and drove towards the wooded area. The judge slowly cruised up and down the streets all around the woods but no sign of the man was found. They returned home disappointed. The judge called the police and demanded that Drew be watched.

Two weeks went by when the judge received a phone call. It was Leti and she was hysterical.

"Calm down," ordered the judge. "What are you trying to say?"

"Drew has disappeared. He did not sleep in his bed last night and I cannot find him anywhere."

"We will be right over," said the judge.

CHAPTER 8
THE ESCAPE

The judge and Daviel got to Leti's house in record time. They went into Drew's room to look for evidence. Satisfied that Drew had not gone for a walk, they called the police. Sergeant Pike came to the house. He listened to the stories about the hit and run driver, the trailing of the different suspects, and the disappearance of the boy.

"Well, ma'am," said the Sergeant. "We really can't do anything until he is missing for twenty-four hours or until you receive a ransom note or phone call. I am sorry. Call us if he does not return in twenty-four hours."

"Wait a minute sergeant. The police were supposed to be keeping an eye on the boy. Where were they?" asked the judge.

"We stopped watching the boy a couple of days ago. We never saw any evidence that the boy was being followed. Sorry ma'am." he said to Leti. "Call us if you hear anything. I am sure he will turn up soon."

After the sergeant left Leti exclaimed, "He thinks Drew ran away! Drew wouldn't do something like that!" She started to cry.

"You know that, and we know that, but the police don't. I guess we will have to wait for a phone call or ransom note," declared the judge.

"Ransom note," repeated Leti. "I have no money to pay a ransom."

"True," stated the judge, "but Daviel does."

Slowly the light dawned on Leti. "I see," she said. Now she knew how her mysterious benefactor knew when she and Drew had needs.

"Why don't you come and stay with us. I am sure that Daviel will receive the ransom note or call and not you. You can leave your house," said the judge, kindly.

* * *

While they waited for a note or phone call, Drew was waking up from sleep. Where am I, he thought. Then he remembered going into his room. After shutting the door someone grabbed him from behind and put a cloth with some sweet-smelling stuff on it over his mouth. Now he was lying on a bed. He only had on his underwear and he was cold. What had happened to his pajama bottoms? He wrapped the thin blanket around him. There was not any heat in the shack. He was glad that this January was warmer than usual but it was still cold. As he lay there thinking about what to do Alan walked in.

"So, you're awake finally. I thought that maybe I gave you too much chloroform and you were going to stay in dreamland forever," he said with a laugh.

Drew did not think it was so funny. "Where am I? My head hurts. What are you going to do to me?" he asked.

"Do, to you," said Alan, "I'm not going to do anything to you but you are going to do something for me.

Drew looked at Alan and said, "I don't think so."

Alan laughed again. "You aren't exactly in a position to make threats little boy. I am much bigger and stronger than you. Maybe you would like for me to break your wrists again."

"So, you admit to running me down in that sports car of yours. Why didn't you stop to help me?"

"You see kid, it was like this: I was drunk and with one more drunk driving arrest my old man said that he would cut me off. I don't know how you and those other two brats found me but my old man chewed me out after the judge visited him. He knew that I was guilty so I admitted it. He came close to disowning me then and there but I persuaded him to calm down. It was fortunate for me that you and your friend couldn't be one hundred percent sure that I ran you down."

"Why are you telling me all this," asked Drew.

"Because you are going to give me your rich friends phone number so that I can call him. I think that three million dollars ransom would do the trick."

"Are you crazy?" asked Drew starting to laugh.

"What are you laughing at?" asked the angry man.

"He won't give you three million dollars ransom for me. We've only known each other since the night you ran me down. Besides that, he may be rich but he's not that rich."

"For your sake kid I hope he pays or don't you know that your red-haired friend is a multi-millionaire?" Alan stepped closer to the boy. "If he doesn't pay the money I'll have to kill you."

Drew, drew back in fear. He was thinking that Alan was crazy. Was Daviel really a multi-millionaire? That would explain a lot, he thought. He gave Alan the number and Alan made the call.

"Hello," said Daviel.

"Listen kid," said a voice. "I have something that you want but it will cost you three million dollars to get it back. You have until Wednesday to get the money."

"How do I know that you have Drew?" asked Daviel.

"Don't worry kid. You can find proof in the hole in the wall by the statue in the park. Don't call the police if you want to see your friend again, alive that is," said the voice before hanging up. Looking at Drew, Alan said, "They will find your pajama bottoms there."

Now he knew why he was wearing only his underwear. "Do you think that I could have another blanket and something to eat? I'm hungry and cold."

Alan looked at the boy, "Sure kid, I'll bring back some food after I send this ransom note."

He tied Drew's hands and feet together behind the boy's back. It was very uncomfortable but there was no way for escape. At least he covered the boy with the thin blanket before he left. Drew was thankful for that.

* * *

The judge had listened to the conversation. "We now know that Drew has been kidnapped." Turning to Daviel he said, "If he calls back we want to speak to Drew to be sure he is all right."

Daviel shook his head yes. Leti was quietly looking at him. "You know dad," started Daviel, "this has to be Alan. No one else would know that we knew about the hole by the wall near the statue. No one else would have any reason to kidnap Drew. No one else would know that we were friends. Let us go to the bank and get the money."

"You're going to pay the man?" asked Leti.

"Of course! Do you not want me to grandma?"

"Oh, yes, I do, but that is a lot of money," she replied.

"Drew is worth a whole lot more than that to me," said Daviel.

Grandma gave him a big hug and said," He is worth more than that to me too."

"I think we should call the police," said the judge.

"But the man said not to," Daviel protested.

"I know that, but the kidnapper needs to be captured and we need advice. Let's go down to the police station and at least talk to Sergeant Pike."

On the way to headquarters they went to the park and pulled a package from the loose stone behind the fountain. They found Drew's pajama bottoms.

"Drew usually only wears those and his underwear to bed," said Leti. "I hope he is somewhere warm."

They went to police headquarters and met with the Sergeant.

"We will come to your house and set up surveillance. When he calls back you need to keep him talking for as long as you can so that we can trace his call."

"This is the plan," began Sergeant Pike. "We want you to put newspapers in a suitcase and pretend that it is the three million dollars. When the kidnapper comes for the "money" we will catch him and make him tell us where Drew is."

"No!" said Daviel. "The man said no police. Drew's life is worth a whole lot more than three million dollars, and besides that; I can afford to lose that and more."

"You do not understand," said Sergeant Pike. "We will surround the kidnapper, capture him and I guarantee he will tell us where the boy is."

"And what happens if you do not capture him or he does not talk. I want my friend back alive!" said Daviel as he left the room.

The judge and Sergeant Pike talked about the different options they had and Daviel made a decision.

That afternoon Daviel said he needed to take a walk. He secretly hailed a Taxi and went to a store.

"Wait here," he told the driver. "I'll be right back."

Daviel bought a big enough suitcase to hold three million dollars, he hoped. He got into the taxi and went to the bank. He entered the bank after telling the taxi driver to please wait.

"May I see the president, please," he asked the cashier.

"Certainly, Master Amberstcrombie; please take a seat while I see if he is free."

A few minutes later Mr. Percival ushered Daviel into his private office.

"What can I do for you," asked the bank president.

Daviel told him the whole story including the part about not paying the ransom. Then he told the manager that he wanted the money on hand in case he had to pay it.

"You must promise me that you will not call my dad and tell him about this money. Drew's life is more important to me than three million dollars."

The bank manager hesitated. What should he do? Daviel was only fifteen years old and the judge was his guardian. True, the judge did say that Daviel could do whatever he wanted with his money and if he made Daviel mad he might put his money in another bank. He felt confident that Daviel could persuade his dad to leave the money in his bank even if the judge got mad.

"Okay," said the manager, "but if I get into trouble with the judge about this you will have to help me out."

"It is a deal!" exclaimed Daviel.

Two hours later Daviel got into the taxi and returned home. He quietly snuck into the back door of the house and hid the suitcase in his bedroom. As he entered the room with the police and their equipment he felt really bad. He did not like going behind the judges back. They waited all day for a phone call but none came. Finally, they went to bed.

Daviel could not sleep and around midnight he woke up the judge. He was upset.

"What's wrong," asked Mrs. McKnight. "Are you worried about Drew?"

He nodded his head yes. "That is not why I am upset though."

He looked at the faces of them both. "I did something bad today." He then told them about the three million dollars in the suitcase in his room.

The judge took him into his arms and held him tight. Daviel sobbed, "We have to pay the money dad. I am afraid that if we don't he will kill Drew. I cannot take that chance. I am sorry I deceived you both. I made Mr. Percival promise not to tell you. Do not be mad at him."

At that moment the phone rang. It was Mr. Percival.

"I am glad that you called," said the judge. "I have an upset young man in my room right now. He just told me the whole story. I do appreciate your call though."

A very relieved bank president hung up.

"Daviel," said the judge. "I wish you had talked to me about this. I would have listened to you."

"I know, but you seemed to be in favor of the plan. I did not know what to do. If there is a next time I promise to talk to you."

"Good!" said the judge. "Tomorrow we will tell the police that you are paying the money. I too was having doubts about the plan. I agree, Drew's life is more important than three million dollars. Now go get some sleep."

* * *

While Daviel was getting the money, Alan was talking to Drew.

"Don't worry kid; your rich friend will pay. I should have asked for five million. Oh well, I'm not greedy, three million will do."

"Why are you doing this," asked Drew. "You said yourself that we could not prove you ran me down."

"That is true, but my contact took pictures of you boys taking pictures of us. He was not happy when he found out your red-haired friend is Judge McKnight's son and now I do not have a source for getting more drugs to sell. You boys cost me a small fortune so I decided that your rich friend would pay. It would take me five years or more to make one million dollars and now I will have three million. I should have asked for more."

"You won't get away with it. They know who you are."

"You are probably right. They probably know who I am but by the time they find you I will be long gone and with a new identity. I already have the fake driver's license, birth certificate, and passport. I have been planning this for weeks. They will never find me.

With your friend's money and what I already have saved I can live like a king."

* * *

The next day the judge and Daviel talked with Sergeant Pike and explained what they wanted. He was not happy but he agreed to do as they demanded. Leti was relieved.

At two o'clock the call came.

"Do you have the money?"

"Before I agree to pay the ransom I want proof that Drew is alive and okay," said Daviel.

"Listen kid, I am calling-the-shots not you."

"Let me talk to Drew or no deal," said Daviel.

There was a pause: "Daviel is that you?" asked Drew.

"It is I," said Daviel. "Are you okay? Has Alan hurt you?"

"No, he hasn't, I'm fine. Don't pay the money —"

Daviel heard a slap. "Listen kid, if you don't want me to kill him, you better have the money."

"I have it," said Daviel. "Where do you want me to deliver it?"

"You will receive instructions in the mail in a day or two," said the caller and then he hung up. The call was too short and could not be traced.

Two days later the ransom note came. The judge and Sergeant Pike read the note. They were to take the money to a deserted road and park at the road's entrance. Daviel was to get on his bike and ride three miles down to the covered bridge. He was to drop the money over the side, pick up the envelope he would find telling them where to find Drew, and ride back to the main road. He had to have the money at the bridge by three o'clock. If he simply took the envelope without leaving the money he would never see Drew again; alive that is.

Looking at his watch the judge decided they could just about make it if they left immediately.

"Whoever the kidnapper is, he sure planned this well. We won't have time to set up a stakeout," complained Sergeant Pike. "Let's go."

They put Daviel's bike in the back of the judge's truck and went to the deserted road. Daviel rode to the covered bridge and left the money. He picked up the envelope and rode back to the truck as fast as he could. He gave the envelope to the judge and Sergeant Pike.

"All units close in, close in, we have the envelope," said sergeant pike into the microphone of his car.

"What are you doing!" yelled Daviel. "Are you trying to get Drew killed?"

"Look kid, you have your job to do and I have mine."

"Come," said the judge to Daviel.

Daviel threw his bike into the back of the judge's truck and jumped into the seat beside him. They followed the directions in the envelope only to find another envelope with more directions. It took them five hours to find Drew in the old abandoned shack. He was shivering with cold.

"Hi guys, what took you so long?" asked a smiling but shivering Drew.

Daviel called grandma. "We have him and are taking him to the hospital to be checked out. Hold on, he wants to talk

to you."

"Grandma, I'm f-fine and I d-don't need to go to the h-hospital," said Drew.

"He is going!" yelled Daviel into the phone.

They took Drew to the hospital where the doctor checked him out. Thankfully, he did not have to enter the hospital in his underwear. Daviel brought some of his clothes for him to put on. Drew had hypothermia from being in the abandoned shack and he had some dehydration but other than that he was okay. They let him go home.

Entering the judge's house his grandmother threw her arms around Drew and cried all over him.

"It's okay grandma. I'm fine. Please don't cry," repeated Drew over and over.

Finally, she let go of him. He was given some hot soup and sent to bed. He and Daviel talked for a little while before they fell asleep.

The next day Sergeant Pike came to the house to see Drew.

"What can you tell us about your abductor?" he asked.

"It was Alan," he said, "but you already knew that." Drew told them the whole story.

"We followed him into the woods but then we lost him. He just disappeared! We will keep on looking for him but with his new identity he will be hard to find. We have sent out an APB on him to the airports, bus terminals, train stations, etc. If he tries to leave the country he will be spotted. Also, his red car should be easy to spot."

"Oh, I forgot. He no longer has the red car. He said that he had other means of transportation."

"I wonder what that means," said the judge.

CHAPTER 9
MOVING AWAY

Hal came back from visiting his dad's friends in Savannah, Georgia to find out he had missed all the excitement.

"I search for months for Alan, and when I go on winter vacation all the excitement happens," he complained. "Did Alan really escape?"

"It wasn't all that exciting," remarked Drew remembering the cold and lack of food. "It cost Daviel three million dollars."

"It was money well spent," said Daviel. "Alan got away clean. The police will continue to look for him for a while. Are you guys ready for school to start back?"

"NO!" shouted the two boys.

From January to March the boys waited to hear some news about Alan but none came. Hal's dad was gone a lot during those months and Hal missed him.

On March 10th, Hal rode his bike to Daviel's house. He was very upset. He didn't knock on the door but rushed right in. The judge, Mrs. McKnight, and Daviel were in the living room watching TV. They could see that something was wrong.

"What's the matter," asked Mrs. McKnight.

"We're moving," cried Hal in anguish. "Dad just told me that next Saturday we would be moving to Savannah. It's not fair!" he cried.

Daviel did not know what to say. He was dumbfounded. Finally, he said, "You cannot move. You are my very best friend. What would I do without you?"

"Calm down," admonished the judge. "Why are you moving?"

"Dad said that he has a job offer that is too good to refuse. He has been talking with this company for the past three months. That is why he has been away so much. I don't want to move," cried Hal.

"You are moving at the end of next week?" asked Mrs. McKnight.

"That's what he said. When he and mom were gone last weekend, they found a house and they already have a buyer for ours. Mister Chinau has wanted to buy it for years so that he would be closer to his sister. I don't want to move!" cried Hal again.

Daviel was still in shock. He was going to lose his very best friend in only a week. What would he do without Hal? Sure, he still had Drew, but Hal was very special. He shared all his feelings and dreams with Hal. Drew was a good friend but no one could ever take Hal's place.

The phone rang and the judge answered it.

"Is Hal there?"

"Yes, he is. He was telling us about the move. Yes, he is rather upset and Daviel isn't doing too well either," said the judge. "Oh, I understand and congratulations on the job offer. Sure, Hal can stay as long as he wants. Why don't you let him stay the night? Tomorrow's Saturday and the boys can play together. I am sure they will want to spend as much time together as they can. Yes, I will explain the situation to them. Good bye."

The judge tried to explain everything to the boys but their broken hearts would not let them understand. They spent every minute they could together. Daviel bought Hal a cell phone so that they would be able to talk to each other whenever they wanted. The week passed quickly, too quickly for Daviel and Hal. It was now time to say goodbye.

The two boys cried on each other's shoulders and had to be pried apart. They were more than just best friends, they were brothers.

Daviel continued to make good grades at school even though his mind was often occupied with thoughts of Hal and not his lessons. The Lord had blessed him with a very sharp mind. He learned things quickly and did not forget them.

Daviel and Hal talked to each other three times a week. The judge and his wife saw the downhearted young man and their hearts went out to him. They had thought that after two months he would have adjusted, but he hadn't.

"I think you should have a man to man talk with Daviel," said his wife.

"About what?" asked the Judge.

"What do you mean 'about what', you can see the boy is still hurting. Maybe he needs someone to talk to but doesn't know how to start the conversation."

"Okay, I'll talk to him."

The judge went up the stairs to Daviel's room. "Hey son, can we talk?"

"Sure dad, what about?"

The judge smiled. He was wondering how to start the conversation. Finally, he said, "Would you like to talk about the problem you are having?"

Daviel pondered the question for a couple of minutes. Which problem was the judge referring to?

"Love hurts," he finally responded. "I do not think that I want to love someone ever again."

"Oh," queried the judge. "Are you having a problem with a girl?"

"A girl!" exclaimed Daviel. "Oh, the new girl is pretty and Sherri is too, but no, I am not interested in a girl right now. Well, maybe as friends. I'll be sixteen soon and well, do you think it is okay to, you know, maybe date more than one girl at a time if they know you are only interested in being friends?"

"Don't try to sidetrack me young man. If it is not a girl that has broken your heart and made it hurt then what are you talking about - love hurts?" asked the judge.

"I am talking about Hal. I gave my whole heart to him and I cannot seem to get over his moving. Several times a day I turn to tell him something and realize that he is not there."

"What about Drew?" asked the Judge.

"Drew is great. We are good friends but he is two years younger than I am and well, he is not Hal."

"The three of you were awfully close before Hal moved," responded the judge.

"Oh, we are still close. I bought Drew a cell phone too and we often have three way calling. I love Drew dad but he is not Hal. Besides that, Drew and Bobby are getting really close. I do not want to interfere with that. Bobby is the same age as Drew. Why did he have to move?"

Judge McKnight wrapped his arms around the boy. He was small for his age and he now looked very vulnerable.

Daviel had matured a lot, both physically and emotionally in the last two years. The judge was often amazed with the decisions that Daviel made like: Using the money God had given him to help others in need and his willingness to pay three million dollars ransom for Drew, and other things. Daviel had a soft, tender heart and that was part of his problem. Maybe it was losing both his parents in an accident when he was twelve that made Daviel so sensitive. Hal and he and Mrs. McKnight had filled that void in Daviel's life for the past two and a half years.

"Why don't we pray about it," suggested the judge.

"I have been praying and it helps some but with summer almost here I do not know if I can stand it without Hal. Maybe we could move away. Then there would not be so many memories," Daviel said looking hopefully at the judge.

"Actually, your mom and I have been talking about buying a smaller house, but son, moving will not solve your problem. Running away never does."

"I know," said Daviel. "I know that time heals all wounds, as the saying goes, and I sure hope mine heals soon."

The judge and Mrs. McKnight continued to support Daviel. School ended and June was almost going too quickly when Hal called Daviel. They had been talking only once a week and that had helped ease their broken hearts.

"Hey, Daviel, how would you like to buy an island?"

"An island?" asked Daviel.

"Yeah, remember when you first inherited all that money, we talked about what you could do with it and you said that you would like to buy an island?"

"Oh yeah, now I remember. Where is this island?"

"It is called Crescent Hook Island and I can see it from my bedroom window. It is one mile off shore." Changing the subject Hal said, "Dad said you could come and spend the rest of summer with us if you wanted to."

"Really!" exclaimed Daviel, all thoughts of buying an island gone from his mind. "Hold on while I go ask dad and mom."

Daviel came back a few minutes later and told Hal, "I guess your parents have already talked with mine. I will be there around four o'clock on Monday."

"I'll meet you at the bus station. By the way, don't mention the island yet. My parents don't even know that it is for sale."

"How did you find out about it?" questioned Daviel.

"I gotta go. I'll tell you all about it when you get here" said Hal before hanging up the phone.

Daviel wanted to choke the life out of his friend. Then he smiled as he hung up the phone. He was going to see his best friend.

Daviel already had his driver's license. The law allowed a boy to get his license one month before his sixteenth birthday if he passed Drivers Ed. He also had a car. Not just any old car but one every boy in

America would like. Because Daviel always showed good judgment and because he was filthy rich; the judge allowed him to by a 1976 Convertible formula 400 Corvette. It was a show piece with all original parts. Daviel did not buy it to drive on a daily basis. He would buy another car for that. The engine had been rebuilt by the previous owner three months ago. (He wanted the best price he could get when he sold it!) It is yellow with a brown top and brown leather interior. The top is automatic with automatic door locks and windows. It is in perfect condition. It is gorgeous!

He bought the car for special occasions and as far as he was concerned this was a special occasion. He did buy a GPS system since he is directionally challenged.

He had the car for only two days when Hal called. He was going to tell Hal all about it but Hal hung up before he could. This would be better he thought. Now he could drive, it was only three hours to Hal's house. He was very excited. Now all he had to do was convince his parents. Today was Thursday. Surely, he could convince them to let him drive on Saturday to surprise Hal.

"Dad," started Daviel as they sat down to dinner, "I was thinking that well, um, maybe I could drive to Hal's house on Saturday. It is only a three-hour drive and I could call you every half hour to let you know that I was okay. P L E A S E!"

The judge with open mouth stared at him then looked at his wife. "What do you think dear?" he asked.

"I don't know. Maybe, if he drove one of our cars and not the corvette it would be all right."

Daviel started to say something then closed his mouth. He figured that at this point silence would be golden. At least he did not receive a flat-out no.

"That is an idea," said the judge. They talked about it for a good ten minutes and then the judge asked, "Daviel would you be willing to drive one of our cars instead of the corvette?"

Daviel's face fell. "I wanted to show Hal my new car but if you would rather I drive one of your cars that would be okay."

They could hear the disappointment in his voice.

"Well then," said the judge, "you can leave on Saturday. How does nine in in the morning sound. That would put you there between twelve and one in the afternoon. Also, you must promise not to drive over sixty miles an hour. I know you are a very good driver but you have never driven for three hours straight before. Is it a deal?"

"Yes sir!" exclaimed Daviel. He decided not to let his disappointment ruin his chance of driving. Hal would have to see his car another time.

"I think," began Mrs. McKnight, "that we should call Hal's parents to let them know you are coming early but that you want it to be a surprise for Hal. They may already have plans for the weekend."

She called and the arrangements were made. All day Friday Daviel was busy packing and making plans. He had two suitcases and an overnight bag. When he came down the stairs with the luggage, the judge asked, "Why the overnight bag?"

Daviel blushed, "I read how the Hardy Boys always carried extra clothes in their car in case of an emergency. I thought I would put some extra clothes in the Vette while I was thinking about it. When I buy the car I plan on driving on a regular basis I will put them in the trunk of that car."

The Judge and Mrs. McKnight laughed. Saturday morning Daviel awoke bright and early. This was the big day. He was driving to his best friend's house three hours away. After breakfast he and his parents went to get the car. As he left the house he saw the Vette parked out front. He looked at his parents with a puzzled expression on his face.

"Your mom and I already had discussed you driving to Hal's house before you asked. We know you are very responsible and a very good driver. We decided that if you would agree to take one of our cars and not the Vette, then we would surprise you with the Vette. I filled her with gas last night. She is all ready to go."

Daviel threw his arms around his parents. "Thank you, thank you," was all he could say. He got in the car, adjusted the seat and mirrors and asked, "May I drive with the top down?"`

"What good is a convertible unless the top is down," said the judge.

Daviel took that to be a yes. He pushed the button to raise the hood. Then he got out of the car.

"What's wrong?" asked Mrs. McKnight.

"Nothing," replied Daviel, "but we need to pray before I go."

They prayed asking the Lord for a safe trip and that Daviel would not have any problems. Daviel got into his car.

"I promise not to drive over sixty and to stay in the right lane if possible and to pull over and call every thirty minutes."

"Good," said the judge. "Hal's parents expect you between twelve and one. If you will be later than that you will need to call us and we will call them. That way Hal won't get suspicious. He might if you call his parents."

"Sounds like a plan to me," Daviel said as he started his car.

Happily, Daviel drove down the interstate. The wind blowing through his hair was exhilarating. Driving his own car, especially one like the Vette was exhilarating in itself. Every thirty minutes he pulled off the highway and called home. He put the car on automatic cruise to be sure not to exceed sixty miles per hour. Surprisingly, there were not a lot of cars on the road. Daviel was ecstatic. The thrill of driving what he thought was the prettiest car on the road and the most powerful car was exhilarating. He had just called the judge after driving for one and a half hours when a policeman pulled him over. He checked his speed before slowing down. He was doing sixty.

"What seems to be the problem officer?" asked Daviel.

"May I see your driver's license young man?" asked the officer.

Daviel started to give the officer his wallet.

"Please take it out of your wallet."

He did and after handing the officer his license he called the judge.

"What's wrong?" asked the judge.

"I just got pulled over by a policeman. I was not speeding. I am using cruise control and I was staying in the right lane. I asked him what the problem was but he did not answer."

"Do you have the pad and pencil that you always carry?"

"Yes sir."

"Good. Write down the policeman's name and badge number. Now let me talk to him."

"Officer, sir, my dad wants to talk to you," Daviel said as he passed the officer the phone.

"This is judge McKnight," explained the judge. "My son tells me you pulled him over. Was he speeding?"

"No sir, this is just a routine check. I noticed the boy and he does look very young and we have had a rash of car thefts so I am checking his registration and everything. Actually, sir, he is a very good driver. I followed him for over a mile. One moment sir -" Returning the officer said, "Dispatch just called and gave me clearance. I am sorry I bothered the boy."

They both hung up. The police officer gave Daviel back his phone and license.

"May I ask why you were writing down my badge number and name?" asked the police officer.

"My dad told me to. Are you related to Officer Johnos in Columbus?" asked Daviel.

"Why, yes I am. He is my kid brother. Do you know him?"

"That is why you look so familiar. He is a really nice man," said Daviel.

"Yes, he is. Sorry to have bothered you, young man. Where are you headed?"

"I am going to Savannah to visit my best friend for the summer. Have a good day officer."

Officer Johnos smiled as the boy pulled away. He decided to call his brother that night to check up on the boy's story.

Daviel stopped and got some lunch. He filled the car with gas even though it was over half full and bought a fountain Pepsi. He was very content.

At a quarter to one Daviel called the judge.

"I am at the corner of Hal's street. I wanted to call and let you know that I got here safely."

"Thanks," responded the judge. "Have a great time surprising Hal and tell everyone that we said hello. We will be down for your birthday. Love you son."

"Love you and mom too," said Daviel and then he hung up.

Now was the big moment. He pulled into Hal's driveway and beeped the horn. He was standing next to the car when Hal came running out the door. He ran right into Daviel giving him a big hug then stood back to look at the car. He stood there with his mouth wide open.

"Wow!" said Mr. Scott.

"Wow!" echoed Mrs. Scott.

"Is it yours?" asked Hal. "When can I drive it? What are you doing here?"

Daviel laughed at his friend and said, "SURPRISE!"

Everyone looked at the car and Daviel explained how he came to buy it.

He parked the Vette in the three car garage and then he and Hal carried his luggage to Hal's room. After putting the luggage on the bed Hal said, "Come here, look!"

"Is that the island?" Daviel asked.

"That's it, Crescent Hook Island."

CHAPTER 10
THE BULLDOG

Daviel looked at the island for a while before saying, "You said you would tell me how you knew it was for sale but your dad did not."

"That's easy," replied Hal. "I was in the library looking at a book. Two men in the next aisle were talking about an island that was coming up for public auction. I knew you were interested in buying an island so I listened. When they said "Crescent Hook Island" I knew I had to call and tell you about it."

"It looks like there is a mansion on it or at least a big house," said Daviel.

"There is an old mansion. It has a lot of rooms. It was remodeled by the previous owner but may need some more remodeling. It was built over two hundred years ago. There is a caretaker and I think the mansion is still in good condition. Let's go ask dad about it."

The two boys went down to dinner. While eating, Hal brought up the subject of the mansion.

"Dad, did you know that the island was coming up on public auction?" asked Hal.

"I heard that rumor —"

"It's not a rumor dad, it's true," cut in Hal.

Smiling his dad asked, "And how do you know it is true?"

Hal told him what he overheard in the library. Then he explained, "I also saw a notice on the bulletin board outside the courthouse. If anyone wants to see it they have to go to the realtors to get a "permission to view" paper."

"Which realtor?" asked Daviel.

"I thought you would never ask," quipped Hal.

He pulled a piece of paper out of his pocket and handed it to his dad.

"Mr. Sorenson at church works there. Maybe he can give us the low down on it. Are you interested in buying it Daviel?"

"Yes, sir, I am."

"After dinner I will call Chuck and see what he has to say about it."

While they ate dinner the two friends talked constantly. Mr. & Mrs. Scott smiled at them. After dinner Mr. Scott called Mr. Sorenson for the scoop on the island. After thanking the man and hanging up he called the two boys.

"Here is the scoop. The island is for sale and yes, we can get a "permission to view" paper tomorrow. The auction is on Monday. It seems the owner has not been paying his taxes and it is being sold. There is a mansion that was remodeled twenty-five years ago and may need more remodeling, but the structure is sound. The roof is only five years old. There is a caretaker on the island and we would need to present him with the "permission to view" paper. He said the minimum bid would be one hundred thousand dollars. I asked him what the island was worth and he said between two million to three million dollars. How does ten o'clock Monday morning sound to you two?"

"You mean we can see it then?" asked Hal.

"That's right," replied Mr. Scott.

Hal gave his dad a big hug.

"Thank you, Mr. Scott. I cannot wait for Monday to come," said Daviel.

The two boys went to Hals room. They had a lot to talk about and a lot of plans to make for the summer.

On Monday they all (including Mrs. Scott) went to get the "permission to view" paper. Mr. Sorenson told them that the auction had been postponed until Thursday. That gave them a little time. When they returned to the Scott's house they got into their boat and headed for the island.

As they neared the far side of the island they were surprised to see the care-takers house with beautiful gardens. A man met them at the dock.

"May I help you?" he asked.

"We have a permission to view paper," explained Mr. Scott.

The man looked at the paper and then gave them the keys to the mansion. They looked all around the mansion, inside and out, and then walked around part of the five-hundred-acre island. They did not explore the whole island, only the areas close to the mansion.

"Where does it get water from?" asked Daviel.

"There is an underground spring. It is really fresh and great for drinking. Water is piped from the well to these houses," explained the caretaker.

"How long have you lived here?" asked Mr. Scott.

Before answering the caretaker's wife came out with ice cold glasses of tea and everyone sat down.

(There was a patio with patio furniture in the center of the gardens.)

"We have lived here for ten years. We love it here."

"What will happen to you all when the island sells?" asked Mr. Scott.

"I guess we will have to move unless the new owners care to keep us on. By the way, my name is Edward and this is my wife Sarah."

"It is nice to meet you. My name is Harold and this is my wife Carol. This is our son Hal and his best friend Daviel."

The boys greeted the couple.

"Are you thinking of buying the island?" asked Sarah.

"Can you keep a secret?" asked Daviel. After they nodded their head yes, he continued. "I am thinking about buying the island and moving here. That is if my parents give me permission and I think they will. I may have to wait a couple of years until I will be eighteen to move, but that would be okay too. If I buy the island I would be honored if you would stay on. There is some work to be done on the house and I would love to learn how to garden."

This pleased the couple immensely. "We promise to keep your secret young man and we hope you do buy the island."

"I hope you buy the island young man and not that awful man that looked like a bulldog. He was absolutely terrible," said Sarah shuddering with the thought.

"We best be getting back home," said Mr. Scott. "It is getting late."

In the boat Hal said to Daviel, "I wonder what she meant by bulldog."

They went back home and Daviel called the judge. He promised that he and Mrs. McKnight would come to see the island the next day. Daviel was so excited.

Mr. and Mrs. McKnight arrived the next day and saw the island and gave their permission for Daviel to buy it. They arranged with the realtor and attorney to put a one million dollar bid on the island. They explained that Daviel wanted to remain anonymous if possible but that he would be at the auction in case he needed to bid higher.

Daviel talked with his parents about moving to the island. He explained that he could have Uncle Jim and his wife move in as the butler and cook and they could watch out for him. He also told them that they could move to the island with him as they were thinking of getting a smaller house. They said that they would think about it.

The auction was an exciting affair. There were not a whole lot of people who could bid for the island but everyone wanted to see who did the bidding.

The auctioneer approached the platform and said, "Ladies and Gentlemen, today we are auctioning off Crescent Hook Island. If you plan to bid, please be sure to register and take a number card. We will start the bidding at one hundred thousand dollars. I do have a secret bid for the island as this purchaser wishes to remain anonymous. If the bidding today is lower than the anonymous bid the island will be sold to the anonymous buyer. We already have his check for the island and we have checked to see if the money is in the bank. It is. The auction will start in ten minutes."

There was a murmur of voices as the auctioneer stepped down.

"How exciting!" exclaimed a lady in the back, "An anonymous buyer."

"How mysterious," said another person.

Soon the auctioneer stepped onto the platform again. A man started the bid at one hundred thousand and soon the bidding was at five hundred thousand.

Two men were raising each other's bid by fifty thousand, going back and forth. Daviel could see the man in the front who was bidding but; who was in the back?

He turned his head to try and see. At the back of the room was a man who just bid five hundred and fifty thousand and he looked just like a bulldog. Daviel grinned and told Hal to look at the man at the back of the room. Hal did and started to whisper something to Daviel but the judge told them both to be quiet.

"Seven hundred fifty thousand going once, going twice, sold," said the auctioneer. Then he added, "To the anonymous bidder." He hit the podium with his gavel and the auction was over. Daviel had bought himself an island.

"Wait a minute!" shouted the "bulldog" marching to the front of the room. "I have a right to know who bought that island."

The auctioneer looked at the man then called the attorney over. All the while the bulldog was hollering.

"If you will just settle down sir," said the auctioneer. "Our attorney can settle this."

"Sir," said the attorney, "I can understand your being upset but I assure you that the secret bid was substantially higher than yours and it is totally legal."

"I have a right to know how much he bid for it," said the bulldog.

"No, you do not," said the attorney. "However, if you would like to raise your bid you may do so at this time. What is your top bid?"

The bulldog looked at the attorney and thought for a moment before saying, "The maximum that I can bid is eight hundred thousand dollars."

"I'm sorry sir but if you had wanted to bid more than one million dollars you would have been closer to the secret bid. Now either leave or we will call the police."

The "bulldog" stormed out of the room shouting, "You haven't heard the last of this!"

CHAPTER 11

FLASHING LIGHTS

Daviel and his party went home to celebrate. The Realtor came to the house and gave Daviel the keys to the mansion. The next day they all went to the attorney's office to sign the papers and then to the island to see the house and to tell the caretakers the good news. They were very happy. The caretakers were glad that the "bulldog" did not get the island.

The next day the judge and his wife returned to their home. During the rest of the week the boys went to the island. Daviel talked with the caretakers about them hiring someone to come in and clean the first floor as he still wanted to remain anonymous.

The "bulldog" reported back to his boss that they lost the island. His boss was angry especially when he found out the buyer was anonymous.

"No matter," said the boss. "We will have to search during the night so as not to be seen. No one else knows the island's secret."

Over the next few days Daviel and Hal explored the mansion. It was dusty so they took a change of clothes, soap, shampoo, and towels so they could shower before going home. They had a great time exploring and they both felt sure that there would be secret passages in the old mansion. They would look for them after Daviel moved in. The judge and Mrs. McKnight gave their permission for Daviel to move to the island but said nothing about moving in with him. They had secret plans of their own.

Entering the front doors there was a grand entryway with stairs on the right and left going to the second floor. At the front and to the left of the doors was the everyday dining room, kitchen, and cook's bedroom and sitting room. Past that on the left was a formal dining room.

At the front, to the right of the front doors were three good sized suites.

At the back to the left was a grand ballroom, two stories high with two restrooms, one for ladies and one for men. Across from the ballroom was a library filled with books. Behind it was a large room that Daviel planned to make into a surround sound theatre/living room.

At the far back of the mansion past the stairs to the right were the rooms that Daviel planned to live in. There was a gigantic bedroom and bathroom and three more bedrooms.

The second floor to the left of the stairs was open to the ballroom with a railing and forty-foot long bench. Down the hall towards the front of the house there were three large rooms. Up the servant's stairs at the back and to the left was a large room that would be used for a servants lounge. To the right of the stairs was a hallway leading to four bedrooms, all with baths. To enter the servant's area, you had to enter via the stairs through the servant's lounge. To the right of the stairs there was a hallway that led to a large linen closet and three large suites. There were also three large suites at the front of the mansion. The front six rooms had doors leading to a twenty foot balcony. The Mansion is three stories high. The first two floors each have fifteen-foot ceilings. The third floor or attic has only a twelve-foot ceiling.

There are fourteen rooms (12 bedrooms) not counting the large linen closet on the second floor with twelve bathrooms. On the first floor there are twenty rooms, seven bathrooms, and three ½ baths. There are a total of thirty four rooms that total thirty-two thousand seven hundred seventy square feet of living space. That does not include the two twenty feet wide porches.

Daviel would have fun decorating and furnishing the mansion. There was a lot of beautiful wood all around the rooms.

All the ceilings were fifteen feet high and all the rooms were large. Behind the ballroom was a large outdoor patio surrounded by beautiful flowers.

The previous owner had remodeled the house twenty-five years ago so Daviel would not need to make any major changes. It was he that installed all the bathrooms. Every bedroom has a private bath!

They spent their days tapping walls trying to find any secret passages. Finally, they gave up and decided that after everything was cleaned up and the remodeling done they would try again. Daviel planned to move the servant's quarters from the third floor to the second floor.

While Daviel and Hal spent their days at the island the "Bulldog" and more of the Boss' workers spent their nights searching the island.

Daviel and Hal had not spent the night on the island yet, but were making plans to do so.

The next day was July 4th and they all made plans to see the fireworks display. That night Hal couldn't sleep so he looked out his window to look at the stars. What he saw surprised him.

Quickly he woke up Daviel. "Wha, what is it?" asked Daviel.

"Look at your island," said Hal.

Daviel looked at the island and was surprised at what he saw. On the far-right side of the island, where the hook was, he saw flashing lights. The boys watched for a while and then went back to sleep after making plans to investigate. Their investigation would have to wait until after the fourth of July. Mr. and Mrs. Scott had big plans for the whole day.

Everyone went to the park to ride the rides and check out the craft booths. Daviel found presents for his mom and dad. He was trying to find something special for Hal when he had an idea. He would buy Hal a new car for his sixteenth birthday. He already knew what type he wanted and the color. They had talked about it for over a year and there was one at the car dealership on the way to church.

The rest of the day flew by and the boys were very tired after the fireworks show. They undressed, jumped into bed and were fast asleep. The next morning Hal wanted to go explore the island. Daviel said that he had something that he had to do and they would have to go tomorrow.

"What are we doing?" asked Hal.

"We, are not doing anything," said Daviel. "I am going somewhere and you are staying here. I have some birthday shopping to do."

"Oh," said Hal. "What are you going to buy me?"

"Naughty boys get nothing," said Daviel as he went downstairs to breakfast. He had secretly made arrangements to meet Hal's dad at the car dealership that afternoon at one o'clock. He would spend the morning looking at some stores and buy a few small things for Hal so that he would not get suspicious.

At one o'clock Daviel pulled into the car dealership. Mr. Scott pulled in behind him. They got out and started looking at cars. Mr. Scott thought that a good used car would be good but Daviel had other ideas.

"Sir, I would really like to buy Hal a new car. Do you see that car over there?" he asked pointing to a car in the front row. "Every time we pass by here on the way to church, Hal drools over that car. He and I have looked at it and I know that he wants it. Could we at least look at it?"

Putting his hand on Daviel's shoulder Mr. Scott said, "Sure, why not, but I do not want Hal to take advantage of you, nor for you to spoil him."

"Why not, he is my very best friend." Then more quietly he said, "He is more like my brother."

Mr. Scott smiled at the boy. He knew how much this boy loved his son and that Hal felt the same way about Daviel.

"Sir," said Daviel hoping to convince Mr. Scott. "Hal has been my best friend for almost three years. After I inherited the money he was my only true friend. He has never asked me for a penny. I really would like to buy this car for him."

Before Mr. Scott could answer a salesman came over.

"Can I help you and your son find anything? My name is John," he said holding out his hand.

"I'm Harold and this is Daviel but he isn't my son. We are looking for a car for my son who will be sixteen on the 18th of July. The car will be a surprise birthday present."

The car had a V-8 350 engine, and was a T-top. It was dark blue with black interior. It already had a GPS system, multiple CD player, air, and automatic. Daviel thought it was perfect for Hal. All he had to do was convince Mr. Scott.

"Could we talk privately for a minute?" Daviel asked the salesperson.

"Of course," he said handing them his card. "If I can help you in any way please come to my office."

"Could we test drive the car?" asked Mr. Scott.

"Certainly, I will be right back with the keys."

After test driving the car they went into John's office to talk. Finally, a deal was made. Daviel wrote a check for the car. The dealership would put the car out front with a sold sign in the window so that Hal would see it when they went to church on Wednesday. On July the 18th they would wash, wax, and fill the car with gas and park it out front. Daviel and Hal would drive to the lot to look at cars. When Mr. Scott drove up John would bring out the keys and hand them to Hal. It was a perfect plan.

Mr. Scott went back to work and Daviel went back to the house. Hal met him at the door.

"Are those for me?" asked Hal looking at the presents in Daviel's hands.

"Maybe, if you are a good boy until your birthday," teased Daviel.

"Do I have to be really good or just so-so good?" Hal teased back.

"You have to be perfect," Daviel said as he entered the house.

"Hey!" yelled Hal, "nobody is perfect."

"Then you can be the first."

All afternoon Hal tried to get his friend to tell him what he bought. That night the boys stayed awake looking out the window to see if the flickering lights were back. They did not see the lights last night because they fell asleep and did not wake up until morning. Tomorrow they would go to the island and scout around.

The cleaners were coming in the morning to clean the first floor so the boys did not want to be around while they cleaned. Mr. Ed said that he hired these people to clean the mansion twice a year. This would be a good opportunity to see what was happening at the hook.

The next morning before the workers were to come the boys packed a lunch and headed for the island. They walked through the woods to the hook. When they got there, they noticed that someone had been digging. Why would anyone be digging here they wondered? The boys decided that they had to spend the night on the island.

"So, do you think that your parents will let you?" asked Daviel.

"If we don't tell them about the lights and digging I don't see why not."

"Hal," said Daviel, "we have to tell them. Maybe your dad would like to check it out with us."

"He may say no," complained Hal.

"Listen buddy, if you cannot spend the night then I will not either. I would really like to find out what is going on but if I have to I will tell the police and they can check it out."

They headed back to Hal's house. Mr. Scott would be home from work soon. At the dinner table Daviel told Mr. and Mrs. Scott about the lights and the digging. He then explained their plan to spend the night at the mansion and spy on whoever was digging.

Mr. Scott thought about it. He looked at the two boys who were small for their size. "I think it would be okay —"

"What!" interrupted Hal's mom. "Are you crazy?"

"Please let me finish dear. I have explored the island and I believe that if you boys hid behind the hill amongst the large bushes you could pretty well see what was going on and no one would know that you were there. If you agree to do that, take your phone with you in case of an emergency, and not try to get closer to the men, I will let you go."

"We promise!" exclaimed the boys in unison.

Mrs. Scott was not too happy about it but she said nothing. She knew that the boys would be careful and not do anything foolish but still she worried.

"I won't sleep a wink tonight," she declared.

"They may not come tonight," said Hal. "They don't come every night.

Hal was right; they did not show up that night so they hid again the next night. They had fallen asleep and were awakened by the sound of voices. Quietly they listened.

"Come on," said a voice, "let's go dig over there. We have to find that treasure and soon before our luck runs out."

"I sure wish I knew who owned this island," said a familiar voice.

Hal whispered to Daviel, "That sounds like the "bulldog"."

Daviel nodded his head. He was wondering what they meant by treasure.

The moon was behind a cloud so they decided to try and get a better look. As they stood up to see better the moon came out. Luckily for them the men were engrossed in conversation and did not notice them. Quickly the boys sat down. It was the "Bulldog". The boys quietly slipped away and called Hal's dad. It was decided that the boys would stay in the mansion and come home in the morning. Hal's dad suggested that they go to the library tomorrow and see what they could find out about the island.

CHAPTER 12
RESEARCH

The next day the boys went home. After breakfast they went to the library. Hal had a library card and Daviel applied for one. He used Hal's address since he still did not want anyone to know that he owned the island.

They asked the librarian where they would find information about Crescent Hook Island. She asked them why they wanted information about that island. They told her that they were curious about it because they could see it from Hal's bedroom window and because of the mysterious owner.

"It sure is funny; you boys are the second person to be interested in that island. Last week a man that looked like a bulldog came in here asking for information. Follow me," said the librarian.

She took them up to the third floor and started pulling out books. "If you boys are interested in islands, you should read this one about Sabertooth Island. I sure wish I knew where that island was."

"How come?" Hal asked.

"If I told you, you would not need to read the book," she spouted. "Boys," she said as she walked away.

The boys spent the next three hours looking for clues as to why anyone would want to dig on the island. The books told about how pirates would use the island because of its secret cove on the hook side. It was interesting reading but they had to get back home. They choose three of the books to check out and the one about Sabertooth Island.

"Why do you want that one?" asked Hal.

"I think it would be interesting and besides I want to find out what she was talking about," Daviel explained nodding his head at the librarian.

After checking out the books they headed home for lunch. Hal's dad decided to take half a day off and he took a book to look through.

After reading all the books, except the one about Sabertooth Island, they found nothing to give them a clue as to why someone would dig on the island. Later that night the librarian called to see if the boys had accidentally taken a rare book about the island home with them. They asked her the name of the book and why it was so rare.

It is called: A True Account of Crescent Hook Island and was written by the first mate on Captain Smythe's ship.

They told her that they only had the ones that they had checked out but that they would keep an eye out for the other one.

After watching some TV, they went to bed. They were tired and did not care if someone dug on the island. Daviel had a weird dream. In the morning he told Hal about it.

He was in a library looking for a rare book but he could not remember the name of it. Just as he found it he was grabbed by someone and knocked out. When he came to the book was gone. He was very disappointed but did not know why. Then he woke up.

Hal said it was not important. He probably had the dream from everything going on in his head, from spying on the bad guys, going to the library, and reading about pirates on the island.

"I do not think so. There was something familiar about my dream. I wish I could remember what it was. Maybe I will remember later."

They did not go to the island that day. The cleaners should finish cleaning the first floor. Daviel wanted to see how good of a job they did before hiring them to clean the rest of the mansion. They spent the whole day playing monopoly. Hal won. They made plans to go to the island the next day.

When they got to the mansion Daviel felt something was wrong. Slowly he opened the door. Everything looked okay. He motioned for Hal to be quiet as they walked towards the library. As they got closer to the library door they could hear someone inside. When they pushed the library door open it squeaked. In the library was a man they had never seen before. They looked at each other; then the man ran out the other library door, and out the back door. They gave chase but could not catch up to him.

"I sure would have liked to have caught that man," said Daviel. "We better go back to the library to see what damage was done."

Entering the library they saw that nothing was out of place except for the book the man dropped when he ran away. Hal started to reach for a book from the section that the man was looking at, but Daviel stopped him.

"Wait, I think we should call the police so do not touch anything. Let us go and talk to the caretaker."

They found Edward puttering in his garden. After explaining what had happened the three of them went back to the library.

"How did he get in?" asked the caretaker.

Hal said that he ran out the back door.

"The back door," whispered the caretaker. "Oh, Master Daviel, I am so sorry. I forgot that the back door lock doesn't always catch when shut. It has not been used in years. If anything important has been stolen I will never forgive myself."

"It is okay," said Daviel "I think that we should call the police and then have that lock fixed."

He smiled reassuringly at the older man as he called the police.

Officer Vicks asked, "Why would anyone want to burglarize the library? I guess there may be some rare books here that would be worth some money," he added.

While the police did their job Daviel and Hal stayed hidden. Edward dealt with the police. The police took finger prints and left.

"Too bad we had this room cleaned," said Daviel.

"How come?" asked Hal.

"If we had not had the library cleaned there would have been more fingerprints and some footprints in the dust. While we are here we might as well check the card catalog for books on Crescent Hook Island."

Daviel found three cards including one for the rare book that was stolen from the library. When he and Hal went to the correct section for the books they were surprised to find that it was the same section that the man was looking at. Hal accidentally dropped a book on the ground and Daviel bent down to pick it up. He stayed down there for a few seconds and Hal noticed a funny expression on his face.

"Hal!" exclaimed Daviel. "My library is the same library that was in my dream. That is why it seemed so familiar. I wonder if that means anything?"

"I doubt it. You know what the pastor said about dreams. They usually are about what we have been thinking the most about. God does not work in signs anymore since we have the Bible. He talks to us from His Word," quoted Hal.

"Hey! That was a pretty good imitation of Pastor John," said Daviel with a smile.

The boys searched for the books but they were not there.

"Do you think the man already found them?" asked Hal.

"He had nothing in his hands when he ran out," Daviel said.

"Maybe they aren't here anymore," decided Hal.

"They have to be here or else there would be empty spaces where they were before," said Daviel.

"Not if they were replaced with other books," surmised Hal.

"That is true," said Daviel, "but then why are the cards still in the card catalog. If someone removed the books then he would have removed the cards too, at least I would have. Maybe they are in another section of the library."

They searched the library for several hours until it was time to go home for dinner. On the way home Hal said, "Tomorrow is Saturday; let's see if dad can come back with us tomorrow. Maybe he can think of something."

At dinner the boys talked to Mr. Scott who agreed to accompany the boys the next day. He was interested to see what the intruder was looking for.

* * *

In another section of town another discussion was taking place.

"What!" shouted an angry man. "We spent all that money bribing that worker to leave the back door open and you leave with nothing."

"But boss, I looked where the card catalog said they would be but they weren't there," whined the man. "It isn't my fault—"

"What!" again shouted the boss. Before the man could say a word, the boss berated him royally. As the man was leaving he mumbled to himself but loud enough for the boss to hear. "It's not my fault if two boys came in and I had to leave."

"What did you say, two boys," asked the boss. "What did they look like? How old were they? Speak up man don't mumble."

"I said they were about fourteen—"

"Both of them or only one of them?" he asked.

"Yeah boss, they both looked about fourteen. One had black hair and the other had red hair."

"Was it a carrot color of red or—"

"No sir," interrupted the man. "It was that really pretty dark red that some girls have only this was a boy."

The boss thought to himself. Could HE have bought the island? "Could he possibly have been sixteen and not fourteen?"

"I, I guess so if he were small for his age."

The boss thought, Daviel was small for his age. It has to be him or why else would two boys be in the mansion unless one of them owned it. But who was the black-haired boy. It could be the other boy in the photos.

"Boss," said the "bulldog". "There was a red-haired boy at the auction who bid once or twice on the island. He was sitting next to an elderly man and a boy with black hair. I thought he was bidding for the judge."

"The judge!" shouted the boss jumping out of his chair. "Why wasn't I told this information sooner?"

"Calm down boss," said the bulldog.

"Don't tell me to calm down you moron. Why haven't you told me this information before now? How do you know the man beside the boy was a judge?"

"It was judge McKnight. I recognized him from photos in the newspaper."

"That's it," said the boss. "So Daviel bought the island. I wonder why? Leave," he commanded. "I have some thinking and planning to do."

* * *

On Saturday the boys and Mr. Scott went to the island. Mr. Scott brought along a flash light in case they needed it.

"This is the section where the books are supposed to be," explained Hal. "We have searched everywhere but cannot find them.

Mr. Scott thought for some time before replying then he said, "Sometimes old houses like this one have secret rooms or passageways. Often they were in a library too."

Excitedly the three of them started to hunt. On this wall of the library there were four-foot-wide sections of shelves from the floor, about three feet high with glass doors. Above these shelves were book shelves filled with books all the way to the ceiling. First, they removed all the books and looked one shelf at a time for a secret lever or button or something to open a secret passageway. They didn't find anything. Next, they removed the books on each side of the section where the books should have been. They again found nothing.

Mr. Scott searched the empty shelves with the glass doors but found nothing. They all stood back to think.

"Mr. Scott, did you search the left side of the shelves or only the right side," asked Daviel.

He said that he only checked the right side because most people were right handed. Daviel's idea was that maybe the button or whatever it was would be on the left side because that would not be the normal place for it. He put his hand under the first shelf and felt along the top toward the back.

"I think I found it!" exclaimed the excited boy. "There is a very tiny bump on the bottom of the top shelf. I will see if it moves."

After trying to slide it in every imaginable direction Hal suggested that he try pushing it up. When Daviel did they heard a click and the bottom shelves slid out with the opening to the left to reveal steps going down underneath the mansion. On the backside of the shelves were more shelves lined with old books. The shelf was about three inches thick and the books were kept behind glass doors. The backs of the books were to the back wall so that they could read the titles. These were the missing books along with some others.

Hal started to go down the steps but Mr. Scott stopped him. "You better let me go first. Who knows what may be down there? I will call you if it is safe to come down."

"I have an idea," said Daviel. "Sir, I think you should close the door and see if you can open it from the inside. If you cannot, then we would be here to let you out."

"That's an excellent idea," said Mr. Scott as he grabbed the leather strap and shut the door. After a few seconds the secret panel opened and he came out. "I think that we can all safely go down."

The three of them entered the stairway and shut the door. Mr. Scott showed them how to open it and then shut it again. The two boys took a turn opening the door just to be safe. They went down the stairs to find a large underground room. In the room they found some beds, books, candles, and other things. They could also feel fresh air but could not see where it was coming from. The room was twenty feet by thirty feet.

"I wonder what this was used for?" asked Hal.

"Maybe it was a Hurricane shelter," said his father. "There are beds and shelves for storing food."

That sounded plausible. They went back through the secret panel after taking the rare book with them.

"If we read this maybe we can find a clue to what those men are digging for," said Daviel.

"Have you read the one about Sabertooth Island?" Hal asked.

"Not yet," responded Daviel. "What if you and I spend the night here? We can bring sleeping bags and camp out in what will be my bedroom. If we sleep here we will not have any distractions and we can read both books tonight."

They both looked at Mr. Scott.

"I don't see any reason why not as long as we make sure the doors and windows are all locked you should be okay."

They checked all the doors and windows, which took a while in the large mansion. Everything was locked including the back door with the new lock so they went home for supper.

Later that evening Mr. Scott took the boys to the mansion. Hal's mom sent food for them and they happily entered the mansion. After a quick search Hal's dad was satisfied that everything was okay and he went back home. The boys locked the front door and went to what would be Daviel's bedroom and settled in for the night.

They spent several hours reading the books, commenting often on different passages.

"Listen to this," said Hal. 'In the secret cave Captain Smythe buried his stolen treasure. He felt that it would be safe there because the only way to enter the cave was by the hidden stairway on the hook.'"

Looking at Daviel he said, "I wonder what 'on the hook' means? It goes on to say that the secret harbor allowed Captain Smythe to hide his galleon from enemy ships and patrols. The secret harbor could only be entered if you knew the correct path to enter it. Many a ship had been wrecked on the sharp rocks below the surface of the water. Do you think Drew knows that one of his ancestors was a pirate?"

"Hal, listen to this. 'After two days of being attacked by a British man of war we managed to sink her but not before sustaining severe damage. We limped our way back to Crescent Hook Island and entered her secret harbor. We followed the beach and climbed to the top of the island. There, on the hook side of the island we buried our chest of gold and jewels by the big, no I won't write exactly where it is buried in case someone else finds my journal.'"

"Well, we now know what they are searching for," said Hal.

"Yeah but, that treasure would have been found years ago by whoever found the journal or the pirates themselves may have come back for it."

Silently they read some more. Daviel's account of Crescent Hook Island ended abruptly with, 'We are under attack and I fear we will be sunk. I am going to jump overboard and try to reach shore. May God have mercy on my soul.' On the last page was written: 'I received this journal from my great grandfather. His father wrote it but died before he could go back for the treasure. I too hunted for the treasure but never did find it. I assume that someone else beat me to it.'"

"I guess that is why those men are searching for the treasure. They must believe that it is still here," said Hal after Daviel read the ending to him.

Daviel lay back in his sleeping bag thinking and soon fell asleep. He dreamed of pirates and secret passages and caves. He awoke the next morning with an idea. Could Crescent Hook Island and Sabertooth Island be the same island?

CHAPTER 13
A FALSE LEAD

Daviel kept the thought that the two islands might be the same island to himself. He wanted some time to look for more information. On Monday they had breakfast and decided to explore where the men were digging.

They walked over to the hook and saw that the men had changed locations. There were freshly dug holes by a large rock, a large bush, and several large trees. In fact, if there was anything that could be classified as large there was a new hole. Daviel was glad that the holes were filled in after being dug. He was glad to be working on a mystery but he wanted to spend time buying furniture for the house, exploring the island, and the hook. Of course, he had the rest of his life to do these things. Mrs. McKnight said that she would help him with the house furnishings. Daviel was glad of that because he had no idea of what to buy. He was having the whole mansion painted an egg shell color. Later he would paint the rooms the colors that he wanted.

The men had been pretty thorough in their search. The boys could not find anything that was big that did not have freshly dug earth by it.

"Hal, what exactly did your book say about the cave?" asked Daviel.

"It said that the cave could only be reached by a hidden stairway on the hook. Why?"

"Let us go over to the hook and look over the side of the cliff. Maybe we will be able to get a clue as to where the hidden stairway is. If we cannot find it we will take the boat to the hook side and see if we can find the cave entrance."

They walked over to the cliff edge and looked over. They saw a beautifully enclosed cove and were awed by the beauty of it.

"Look at that!" exclaimed Hal. "It is beautiful. We have to go down there and explore."

"We will," said Daviel, "but first we need to find the hidden stairway and the cave. There is a chance that the treasure has not been found."

"Daviel, my friend, I think you are a little mixed up. The hidden stairway and cave are on Sabertooth Island and not Crescent Hook Island."

"Look at that hook," Daviel said. "Does it not sound like what you read about Sabertooth Island. Does it not seem funny to you that both books talk about Captain Smythe? I think that maybe Sabertooth Island is Crescent Hook Island. It may have had two names."

"You could be right. Their descriptions sure do sound a lot alike. Too bad we didn't find a map showing where the buried treasure was. Do you think that there are two treasures?" asked Hal.

"It sure sounds like it. I would say that the treasure about Crescent Hook Island was found long ago but the hidden stairway and cave may not have been found and that treasure is still there. That is what I am counting on. Come on, let us go get the boat."

The boys made their way to the boat dock.

"There is a way that we could prove that the two islands are the same," said Hal.

"How is that?"

"We could swim in the cove and if there are rocks close to the surface, but out of sight, that would indicate that the islands are the same."

"Hey, that is a good idea. It is about time you started using that brain of yours; I was getting worried about it rusting."

"Very funny," said Hal. "I do have a good idea once in a while."

"Tell you what," Daviel said. "We will look for the cave today and tomorrow we can swim in the cove. We will have to walk along the beach though because we do not want to wreck the boat on the rocks."

"Sounds like a plan to me," said Hal.

The boys spent a couple of hours searching for the cave but they could not see it anywhere.

"We may be able to see it in winter when all the leaves fall off the trees," said Hal.

"Winter, I do not want to wait for winter. Let us go to the library. I want to see if I can find any more information about Crescent Hook Island. Maybe one of the other books will have a map or clue to where the treasure is. We can ask the librarian about it."

They went back to Hal's house for a quick snack and then on to the library. Daviel returned the books he had checked out and asked if the rare book had been found. It had not.

That night as they were watching the news the reporter said, "And now some news about the new mystery owner of Crescent Hook Island. An unidentified source claims to know the owner. He said he is a sixteen-year old boy with red hair named Daviel. Daviel, if you are watching tonight please contact us to verify or disclaim ownership of the island."

"Who could possibly know that I own the island?" asked Daviel.

No one had an answer.

"What should I do?" Daviel asked Hal's dad.

Before he could answer the phone rang. It was the judge. He wanted to speak to Daviel.

"Hello son, it looks like the cat is out of the bag."

"Yes sir, but how did someone find out so quickly?"

"Who knows," responded the judge. "I think you should call the press and let them know that you are the owner of the island and that you want to schedule a news conference to answer any questions. Schedule it for the day after tomorrow. Mom and I will be there tomorrow."

"Okay," said Daviel and hung up. "Dad said I should call the press and schedule a news conference for the day after tomorrow. He and mom will be here tomorrow."

Daviel did call the news station and soon the announcement was made that there would be a news conference with Daviel the day after tomorrow at two o'clock.

Daviel was not happy about the news. He was glad that he had gone to the library already for the books. He and Hal spent the evening looking at them. In one of the books Hal found a map of the island with an X on it. The boys decided to check it out tomorrow. It was near where someone had been digging but closer to the far side of the hook. Neither boy remembered anything big over there but decided to check it out tomorrow. They would bring digging equipment with them.

The next morning their plans were rudely interrupted. When they opened the door to leave the house they were met by several reporters. Cameramen were trying to take their photos in hopes of being the first to air a picture of Daviel.

Quickly the boys returned to the house. They had to stay inside all day and could not go to the island to search. That would have to wait until after the news conference. Every time anyone looked out a window their photo was taken. At one o'clock the judge and his wife drove up. As they walked to the front door all they said was 'no comment.'

"How long have they been here?" he asked.

"They were here early this morning. When Hal and I tried to leave to go to the island at eight thirty they were already there. I do not know how they found out where I was."

"It was your library card," said Hal.

"My library card?" asked Daviel.

"Yup," said Hal with a grin. "The only thing that has this address on it and your name is the library card. I bet the librarian saw the news clip and called the station. How many boys do you know that are called Daviel?"

"Sometimes Hal you amaze me," said Daviel. "That has to be it."

Hal was pleased by his friend's praise. Daviel was the smarter of the two and sometimes Hal felt inferior to his friend although Daviel never gave him any reason to. They stayed in the house all that day and the next until time to leave for the news conference.

Daviel was extremely nervous at the news conference. He was glad that the judge was there with him. It was almost time to start. Hal and his family were sitting on the front row and Hal gave Daviel a thumbs up. Daviel smiled.

"Good afternoon," said the news castor. "My name is Alex Shields and I will be hosting today's news conference. With me on the platform are Master Daviel Amberstcrombie and his guardian Judge McKnight. How are you two today?"

"Fine," squeaked Daviel. Then again, "Fine but a little nervous."

"There is no need to be nervous. I will ask you a few brief questions and then we will open it up to the reporters for further questions. Remember, you do not have to answer any questions that you do not want to. Judge, how are you today? Are you nervous?" asked Alex jokingly.

"I am fine and no I am not nervous. As you said I am the boy's guardian and I am here to give him advice about any questions that I think are irrelevant."

After getting some background history about how the judge was Daviel's guardian and what Daviel was doing here, Alex asked the important question. "Why did you buy the island secretly?"

"I can answer that," said the judge. "When Daviel first inherited his money, he was bombarded with people who wanted to be his so called "friend". I was afraid that if everyone knew that he, a boy of fifteen, bought the island, that he would be bombarded again by false friends who only wanted money from him and not his friendship, so I counseled him to buy the island secretly."

"Just how much money did you inherit?" asked Alex.

The judge started to say something but Daviel stopped him.

"I'll answer that dad, enough to buy the island."

Everyone laughed.

"I see you are a smart young man," said Alex.

"The judge taught me well," Daviel said smiling.

There were several questions about his plans for the island. After that the reporters were allowed to ask questions.

"Would you say that you inherited millions of dollars," asked one reporter.

"No sir, I would not say that. If I wanted you to know how much I inherited I would say I inherited such and such dollars, not millions of dollars."

Again, everyone laughed. Alex requested, "Please no more questions to try and trick the young man into revealing his net worth. Obviously, he does not wish to reveal that information."

A woman reporter asked, "Were you aware of the rumor of lost treasure on the island before you bought it?"

"No, I was not but I have since read some books about that. It seems to me that after all these years that surely the treasure has already been found."

"How do you plan to protect the island from treasure hunters?"

"Until now I did not think there was a need so I really have not thought about it. I think that I will install some surveillance equipment or maybe buy some attack dogs. The island is privately owned and trespassers are not welcome."

"When is your sixteenth birthday?"

"I will be sixteen on July 21st."

"Judge, are you sure he is as old as he claims. He looks quite a bit younger than sixteen to me."

"Yes, Daviel is young looking but he will be sixteen soon."

"Do you have a girlfriend?"

"Not at this time. It is funny that you asked that. Dad and I had that conversation recently. I think that I would rather date several girls as friends right now. I am not looking to get married anytime soon and do not want to give a girl the wrong impression that I am."

"Have you been bothered with a lot of young ladies wanting your attention?"

"Until now, the fact that I am rich has been kept a secret, at least here in Savannah. When I first inherited the money a rash of mothers with their daughters pestered me but now life has pretty much settled down. Oh yeah, about the girlfriend question, I am a born again Christian and would only consider going out with sincere Christian young ladies."

"Are you a snob?"

"A snob, I do not think so, oh you mean because of my previous answer. No, I am not a snob. However, the Bible says that Christians are to date only fellow Christians and I must obey the Bible"

"Our time is running short so I will ask Daviel one last question. "Why did you buy an island?"

Smiling Daviel said, "When I first inherited the money my best friend and I talked about what we would do with the money. One of the suggestions was to buy an island. When my best friend heard about

Crescent Hook Island being up for auction he called me and I came to look at it and bought it."

"Thank you for coming in today Daviel. Judge, it seems your son didn't need a lot of help from you after all."

"No, he didn't and I am very proud of him."

As the judge and Daviel left reporters shouted questions at them hoping Daviel would respond. He didn't.

The next few days, reporters hung around and Daviel would wave at them but he refused to answer their question. Soon they got tired of being ignored and he and Hal returned to the island to check out their new clue.

"Daviel, if you think that the treasure has already been found then why are we going to look for it?" asked Hal.

"I think that there is a good chance that the treasure has already been found but maybe it has not, so; let us try and find it. Besides, the map at the back of that last book looks promising."

"Don't you think that someone else would have already searched there?"

"That is possible but it will not hurt to look."

They went to the spot indicated by the map. No one had been digging in this area because there was nothing big nearby. As they cut through some undergrowth they came upon the stump of a giant tree. This tree must have been bigger than all the other trees they had seen.

Eagerly the boys began to dig. Maybe the treasure was here. They dug a hole two-feet deep all around the stump. They decided to go down two feet more and then quit. As they neared the end of the circle Hal exclaimed, "Daviel I hit something!"

Quickly the boys dug out a chest. It was rusty with age but did not have a lock. They lifted out the chest to open it. It was too small to contain a large treasure. What would they find inside?

"You open it," said Daviel. "You found it."

With shaking hands Hal took the box and opened it up. Inside they found a note. It said, "HA, HA, I fooled you!"

The boys looked at the hole they had dug and broke into laughter. The note was signed, Boyd, First mate on Captain Smythe's Ship, The Sea Ghost.

"That sure was a false clue," said Hal.

"True," said Daviel, "but it does let us know that there was treasure buried on the island at one time.

It could still be here. We will have to look for more clues. If he knew all the work that we put into finding his treasure I bet he would be laughing his head off right now. Let us fill in this hole and go home and tell everyone our story."

"Should we put the note back?"

"No, we will bring that as proof that we are not making it up. The note and chest are very old. Who knows, they may be worth some money."

CHAPTER 14

THE CAVE

The boys took the note and the chest to Hal's dad. He was impressed with their sleuthing abilities and praised them. They told him their thoughts and plans for future sleuthing. He thought that their ideas about Sabertooth Island and Crescent Hook Island being the same island sounded logical.

"What are you boys going to do tomorrow?" asked Mr. Scott.

"Tomorrow we plan to buy some underwater goggles and then walk along the shore to the hook and see if there are dangerous rocks under the surface of the water," explained Hal.

"We figure," interjected Daviel, "that if we find some underwater rocks and a space big enough for a clipper ship to pass through without being wrecked, then the islands are the same island. After we have that proof we will then spend time looking for the hidden stairway"

"That sounds logical," responded Hal's dad. "It sounds like you boys will have a big day tomorrow. You might want to turn in a little early. Oh yeah, before I forget, have you seen any more lights at night, recently?"

"No sir," said Hal. "We think that they may have left for a while. We don't know why though."

"From what we saw," said Daviel, "they seem to have dug everywhere there was anything big, so maybe they have given up. I sure do hope so."

"Me too!" stated Hal. "Good night dad."

"Good night boys."

The boys went upstairs to get ready for bed. They were tired from all the digging they had done and after taking showers they quickly fell asleep. Early the next morning they awoke refreshed and ready for action. They ate breakfast and went to the store and bought underwater goggles. Soon they were at the island.

They walked along the shore to the hidden cove and stripped off their clothes. Hal started running for the water but Daviel stopped him.

"You better not jump in Hal. Who knows what is under the surface of the water. You may hit a rock or something."

Carefully the boys entered the water. "Hal, I think that you should swim out to the center of the hook since you are a better swimmer than I am and I will search the area closer to shore. Call me if you find anything and I will call you."

Hal started swimming to the other side of the hook while Daviel searched closer to the shore. Neither boy saw the man with binoculars high up on the cliff edge watching them. The man wished that he could hear what the boys were saying.

The water was totally clear of rocks where they were searching so they swam closer to the entrance of the hook. The goggles enabled the boys to swim underwater with their eyes open.

Thirty minutes later:

"Daviel, come here!" shouted Hal waving his arms.

Daviel swam out to Hal.

"Be careful," warned Hal. Taking Daviel's hand he said, "Follow me," and then dived under the water pulling Daviel with him, who had just enough time to take a deep breath. Underneath the water about ten feet below the surface was the top of a jagged rock. After touching it Daviel surfaced.

With a big grin he said, "Let us swim under the water and see if there are more of them."

The boys dove under the water. As they found more rocks they would surface to report the new discoveries. They traced a line of rocks that ran from the far side of the hook to the inland part with a space large enough for a clipper ship to pass through. They also found more rocks on the hook side of the island. Any ship hitting those rocks would definitely be sunk. Quietly the boys swam back to a large rock on the shore, climbed onto it and lay on their backs gasping for breath.

"Let us lay here until we dry off. Then we can go for our clothes," said Daviel.

That was fine with Hal. They were not use to swimming and were exhausted.

The man on the cliff could clearly see the boys lying on the rock. He looked at their faces and again wished that he could read lips.

Daviel turned to Hal and said, "That clinches it, the islands are the same."

Hal could hear the excitement in Daviel's voice. He too was excited. "After we are dry, where should we start our search for the hidden stairway?" he asked.

They sat up and looked at the long shore. The hidden stairway could be anywhere. It would take a couple of days to search. They were now dry and put on their clothes and shoes. They decided to search the far end of the hook first. Unfortunately for the man on the cliff, the cliff hung over the shore and he could not see what the boys were doing.

Daviel and Hal searched all along the shore until it was late. They were so intent on what they were doing that they did not realize that lunch time had passed and it was now close to supper time.

Looking at his watch Daviel exclaimed, "Hal, do you know what time it is? It is almost six o'clock. We had better go home before your dad sends a search party out for us. We will have to search again tomorrow."

They walked the shore to where they docked the boat. At least tomorrow they could bring the boat into the cove since they now knew where the dangerous rocks were.

As they entered the house Hal's dad called to them. "So, how did it go?"

They explained about their day and then complained that they were starving since they missed lunch.

At dinner Hal's mom asked, "Daviel, when do you plan on moving into the mansion, not that you are not welcome here because you are, you can stay here as long as you like, I mean, I am not trying to get rid of you or nothing like that but —"

"I understand," interrupted Daviel. "I talked to Uncle Jim and he and Aunt Chris will be here on Friday. The bottom floor is ready for me to move in but I thought that I would wait until they got settled first. Tomorrow is Wednesday and next Wednesday is my birthday so I figure that next Thursday I will move in. Mom and dad are coming for Hal's and my birthdays and mom has promised to help me look for furniture. Hal and I have been so busy trying to solve this mystery that I really have not thought about anything else."

"You do understand that you are welcome to stay as long as you like," said Mrs. Scott. "I didn't mean for it to sound the way it did."

"Of course, the boy knows he is always welcome here don't you son."

"Oh, yes sir, this is my second home and you are like my parents," said Daviel smiling.

"Good!" exclaimed Mrs. Scott.

That evening the boys and Mr. and Mrs. Scott discussed their plans for the next day. Mrs. Scott suggested that they take a sack lunch with them. The boys seconded the idea. They watched a little T.V. and then went to bed.

The next morning Mrs. Scott prepared breakfast and a sack lunch for the boys. They left for the island about nine thirty and promised to be home by five since it was a church night.

They docked the boat in the cove and moored her to the large rock. They spent the morning searching for the hidden stairway and at twelve thirty they decided to take a swim to cool off before eating lunch. The man was once again on the cliff watching them. After their swim they sat on the big rock to dry off and ate their lunch.

"You know Hal, I think we should try over there," said Daviel pointing to an area farther down the shore. "Unfortunately, we will not be able to finish searching the whole shore today."

"Why don't I go one way and you another. That way we could cover more ground," suggested Hal.

They had been searching together and the boys decided that it was a good plan. They would call out if they found anything. After a couple hours of searching, Hal shouted for Daviel to join him. Again, the man on the cliff wished that he could see what the boys were doing. He hoped he wasn't wasting his time watching them.

"What did you find?" asked Daviel.

"Look at the big rock," exclaimed an excited Hal. "Now watch when I push against it."

Hal pushed against the rock and it moved. They decided to get a stick and try to push the big rock away from the wall. It took them almost an hour but finally the big rock moved far enough for the boys to squeeze through. Behind the rock was a little tunnel which the boys followed until it came to an end. They were very disappointed and decided to call it a day after they pushed the rock back into place before going home.

They showered, had dinner and went to church. After church they all went out for ice cream.

The next day Hal said, "Why don't we look for the cave again. Let's take the boat out and look around the outside edge of the island. It has to be there somewhere."

"Let us spend the morning looking for the hidden stairway. If we haven't found it by lunch time we can look for the cave," said Daviel.

They agreed to this plan and once again returned to the cove to search. At twelve o'clock they decided to take a swim to cool off. While lying on their favorite rock to dry off Daviel suddenly hit Hal's stomach.

"Hal, look up on the cliff. I think I saw a man with binoculars watching us."

"What!" said Hal sitting up to get a better look. "I don't see anything."

"He was there a minute ago. I saw the sun reflected on the lens of the binoculars. I wonder how long he has been watching us. We had better get dressed and get out of here."

"What? Aren't we going to look for the man?" asked Hal.

"Not right now. There may be others with him," explained Daviel.

The boys quickly dressed forgetting about lunch. They left the cove and went back to Hal's house. Hal's dad was home from work early and the boys told him what they think Daviel saw.

After eating their lunches and waiting for a couple of hours the boys and Mr. Scott took the boat to look for the cave. They decided to circle around the island in hope of spotting an opening. After their first pass they remembered that the cave had to be near the hook. Slowly they cruised around the hook side of the island. The sun was setting when Hal shouted.

"Look up there," he said pointing. "Daviel, remember where we dug around the big tree stump"

"Sure!"

"Look there and then down about thirty yards. You can just make out an opening in the side of the island."

"I see it!" exclaimed Daviel. "If we can get in the cave we could find the hidden stairway."

"You won't get in the cave that way," said Mr. Scott. "That side of the island is way too steep and there are too many trees and bushes to repel down. And besides that, I saw your man. He ran away when Hal pointed to the cave. He probably thought that Hal was pointing at him."

"How will we get into the cave if we cannot repel down?" asked Daviel.

"It is getting late and that is a problem for tomorrow," said Mr. Scott. "At least we know that there is a cave."

"What about the man?" asked Hal. "Aren't we going to look for him?"

"That too is a problem for another day," replied Mr. Scott.

CHAPTER 15

THE TREASURE

Entering Hal's bedroom Hal's dad said, "I have an idea; with all the excitement about the hidden treasure you have not explored the secret room. Maybe there are some more secrets in the room that might tell you where the hidden stair way is. Why don't we all search there tomorrow until your aunt and uncle arrive?"

"You mean you can help us tomorrow. You don't have to work?" asked Hal.

"Nope! I took tomorrow off."

"Yippee!" shouted Hal. "Do you think that maybe we could look for some clues about who that man is that was watching us?" asked Hal.

"I don't think it would be worth the time. I am sure that he is long gone by now. However, if we see him we will give chase. Okay?"

"Okay," agreed Hal.

The boys stayed up late discussing the mystery even though they would only have the morning to work on the problem because Daviel's aunt and uncle were coming. They would have to help them get moved in during the afternoon.

The next day the three of them headed for the island. They left early because Daviel's aunt and uncle would be there around two. They carried flashlights with them so that they could see since there was not any electricity in the hidden room. Daviel opened the secret passageway and they climbed down the stairs.

They looked around the room with their flashlights and this is what they saw. The room was about twenty feet by thirty feet. On the back wall were four sets of bunk beds, three beds high for a total of twelve beds. Along one wall were books and some games. In the center of the room were some tables and chairs and on the right, by the back wall, was a sunken chest that could be used to keep food cold.

Under one of the mattresses of the beds they found a handwritten diary. It dated back to the Civil War. Could this room have been part of the underground-railroad? They sat down at a table and carefully opened the old book. It told the story of a young black boy named Booker Lee and his family. They had been slaves and were treated badly by the master. Booker Lee was twelve years old. He had three younger sisters and his mother. His father had been sold several years before and they did not know where he was.

Booker Lee explained that they were slaves on a plantation near Savannah and how a Christian man helped them to escape to the underground-railroad. They would spend two days at the mansion and leave the next night when the boat came for them.

The mansion owner told them that many slaves had passed through his home and he hoped that many more would come. He said that his island provided a safe escape from the slave catchers.

"Wow!" exclaimed Daviel. "Just think, my house was on the underground-railroad. I will have to do some more reading about the railroad."

"I wonder why Booker Lee left his diary behind," said Hal.

"Who knows," said his father. "Maybe they had to leave earlier than planned and he forgot it. Whatever the reason, it is a very valuable find. Let's explore some more. Maybe we will find other items of interest."

"You know," said Daviel, "the other owners of this mansion must not have known about this secret room or they would have found the diary. I hope they did not know about the cave, hidden stairway, and the treasure too."

They spent some time looking under mattresses and under the beds but did not find anything else. They sat at one of the tables and talked. They decided to read the diary later.

"What are you looking at Hal," asked his dad.

"Do you see that rope hanging down by the stairs?" he asked pointing to it. "I was wondering why a rope would be hanging there."

They all got up to inspect the rope. You could barely see it as it blended in with the walls and it was behind the stairs they used to get into the secret room.

Mr. Scott pulled on the rope and again they heard a click. This time part of the wall moved. As they pushed it further open they saw a spiral stairway going up. Quickly the boys and Mr. Scott climbed the spiral stairs. They stopped at the top.

"That must be the second floor," said Hal's dad. "Can you see how to open the door?"

The stairs led to the second-floor floorboards. The two boys tried to open the floor but had no luck.

"I wonder where this leads," said Daviel.

"Here, let me try," said Mr. Scott.

He shone his light around the floorboards and noticed a slight gap between the floor joists and the floorboards. Reaching up he slid his hand along the boards first one way and then another. A two-foot square section of boards slid to the left side revealing a hinged door.

He opened the door and went through the opening. He found himself standing in what must be a closet. He helped the two boys up and slid back the bottom floor and shut the trap door. If you found the trap door and opened it you would think that the passageway had been boarded up. It was ingenious.

Opening the closet door, they entered a good-sized room off the back stairs. They went down the stairs to the first floor. It was twelve thirty so they had to leave for lunch.

After lunch, while waiting for Daviel's aunt and uncle to arrive, the boys went up to Hal's room. Daviel was reading the diary.

"Hal, listen to this! 'Mr. Lewis showed us how to access the tunnel from the secret room. He said that it would lead us to a hidden stairway and that would lead us to a hidden cove where the boat was waiting.'"

The boys jumped and shouted for joy. Hal's dad ran into the room.

"What happened!"

"Listen to this," said Daviel and then he read the paragraph.

"Amazing!" said Mr. Scott. "Too bad we don't have time to explore. Jim and Chris just drove up. I was coming upstairs to tell you when I heard the commotion."

They went down and greeted Jim and Chris.

"Oh Daviel, I am so excited and cannot wait to see your island," said Aunt Chris.

"We have talked about nothing else since you invited us to live with you. I like the idea of being the butler and you know how good a cook your Aunt Chris is."

"Yes, sir," said Daviel. "The mansion has been cleaned, top to bottom, and painted an eggshell color. I plan to install carpet and add color to my living quarters. You can change the color in your living quarters if you want to and you will need to pick out carpets. I thought that you might like to do that yourself."

"Hey, don't we get a hug or something," said a voice Daviel recognized.

"Mom, Dad!" exclaimed Daviel. "I thought you were not coming until tomorrow."

"We talked with Jim and Chris and decided to follow them down. We wanted to see our boy and hear what you have been doing," said his Dad.

"Well let's not stand out here and talk," said Mrs. Scott as she led everyone inside.

Daviel and Hal shared all of their adventures with everyone. Everyone was excited to hear about the tunnel and all the rest of the news.

"After all the furniture is unloaded maybe you and Hal can explore the tunnel and tell us about it tonight. We can arrange everything," suggested Aunt Chris.

"Could we!" the boys asked in unison. Everyone laughed at the expectant looks on their faces.

"Sure," said the judge.

"We only brought the antique furniture and the good pieces. We sold everything else," explained Aunt Chris. "What won't fit in our living quarters Daviel, you can put somewhere else. Have you started decorating the mansion yet?"

"No ma'am. Mom said that she would help me so I was waiting for her. I plan to move into the mansion on Thursday, the day after my birthday."

They all went out to unload the U-Haul onto the waiting barge. After three hours everything was carried into the house. While the adults sorted out where everything would go the boys entered the secret room. Using their flashlights, they looked around.

"Where do you think the secret door is?" asked Hal.

"I would guess that it would be on that wall since there are beds on that wall, the stairs on that wall, and the underground box on that wall. Let us look in that corner."

Knowing that there was a secret door and tunnel narrowed down their possibilities considerably. It could only be on the wall they were searching. They pressed, pushed, and touched all along the wall but nothing happened. They searched for thirty minutes. Hal suggested that they look in the diary for a clue. After reading it they found none. They stood in front of the wall staring at it. They could feel fresh air entering from the wall and traced their hand around the wall. This revealed a three-foot wide by six-foot high rectangle where they could feel a slight breeze.

"That has to be the door," Hal surmised.

They narrowed their search to within that area but found nothing. In frustration, Hal leaned his head against the connecting wall. When he leaned his head back against the wall the door started opening. Hal hit his head on a rock which slid back to open the door.

Excitedly the boys pushed the door open. They put a table in the doorway so that the door would not shut. They did not want to take the time to find out how to open the door from the other side as it was getting late. They wanted to explore the tunnel.

The tunnel was three feet wide and six feet high and was lined with bricks and huge timbers. The floor was smooth so they ran down the tunnel. Eventually they came to a dead end. Where was the cave?

They realized there must be another door. The way to open this door was not even concealed. They pulled back the bolt and opened the door and once again propped open the door with a large stone.

They entered the cave. It was huge. As they explored it with their flashlight they found the hidden stairway. It was at the cave entrance. The top of the cliff covered it making it impossible to see it from the cliff. Slowly the boys descended the stairs. At the bottom they found that it too dead ended. How did you exit the stairway?

Quietly the boys stared at the wall. Looking around they noticed a small sliver of light at the top. Daviel reached up his hand and pushed. The top moved up. He and Hal stood on some rocks and looked out. When they did they saw the back of a man looking away from them. Quietly they looked around to get their bearings and then shut the "door".

They returned to the library being sure to shut all the doors. They ran into the kitchen and told the others about their discovery.

"Tomorrow, we will dig for the treasure," said Daviel. Quickly he added, "That is if it is okay."

The adults were as excited about their discovery as they were. The boys helped move some furniture around and then leaving Jim and Chris to get settled in they all went to Hal's house. Daviel had bought some food and stocked the kitchen. Aunt Chris could buy the other things that she needed later.

"If I had set up the mansion instead of trying to solve the mysteries you could stay there," said Daviel to his parents. "I am sorry."

"Let's hear none of that young man," said Mrs. Scott. "The judge and Mrs. McKnight will stay here with us. We have two extra guest rooms and what good are they if they are not used?"

The adults spent the evening talking. The boys went to bed early so they could get up early to start digging.

As he was drifting off to sleep Daviel said, "I wonder who that man was that we saw? He looked familiar. Do you not think so?" he asked his friend but Hal was fast asleep.

Early the next morning they made their own breakfast and left a note telling the adults that they had left. They went to Ed's storage shed and got some shovels and pick ax. Nothing on the island was ever locked.

They walked along the shore and went to where they judged the secret entrance to the hidden stairway would be. They kept a sharp eye out for the man but they did not see him.

They opened the "hatch" and dropped down into the hidden stairway. No wonder we did not find it, thought Daviel.

They climbed the stairs and upon entering the cave Hal asked, "Where should we start digging?"

Daviel looked around and thought. "I have an idea. This cave is located about where we were digging around that big tree. You can see a root on the roof of the cave. I also think that right below that big root would be about the same spot on the map we found. This I think would be the same spot but instead of digging above ground we needed to be digging here in the cave."

It sounded good to Hal so they started digging. After an hour of easy digging Hal yelled excitedly, "Daviel I hit something!"

Daviel helped Hal dig around what seemed to be a metal chest. As they lifted out the heavy chest using the shovel handles as crowbars and dragging it over the edge of the hole they saw that the lid was not locked. Maybe someone else had already found the treasure.

"Open it," said Hal.

"No, you get the honors Hal, you found it."

Hal was shaking from excitement. Slowly he opened the chest. Inside were gold coins, jewels, a jeweled dagger and a jeweled crown. "Wow!" exclaimed the boys.

They did not have time to dig down into the treasure to see what else was there.

"Wow is right," said a voice behind them. "Thank you for finding this for us Daviel."

Turning, the boys looked at the face of Alan Mecham.

"What are you doing here?" asked Hal.

"I have been spying on you for days. I figured you were looking for the treasure too though I don't know how you knew about this cave and the hidden stairway, I sure didn't. Oh well it doesn't matter. Tie them up."

Daviel and Hal both jumped out of the reach of the men but their escape was to be short lived. The men were so much bigger than the two boys that their struggles were in vain.

Quickly the "Bulldog" and two other men subdued the boys and firmly tied them up. They did not gag them since no one could hear them if they screamed.

"You cannot take that," said Hal. "It belongs to Daviel."

"There you are mistaken. I believe the treasure belongs to whoever has it and sorry boys but it looks like I have it," said Alan with a laugh.

"Mr. Mecham, did you tell the press that I was the owner of the island?"

"I sure did."

"How did you find out it was me?"

Alan told the boys the story. "Well so long boys. I guess someone will eventually find you, that is, if you told anyone how to find the hidden stairway. How did you find it yourselves? It is very cleverly hidden."

The boys remained silent. Alan knew they were not going to answer.

"What happened to your ears and nose?" asked Hal.

"I used part of the money Daviel paid me to have my nose and ears made smaller. It is very becoming, don't you think?"

Hal and Daviel could hear Alan laughing as he and his men stole the treasure. They were mad at themselves for not telling the adults how to enter the secret tunnel. They tried to untie their bonds but it was hopeless. How long would they have to wait before being rescued?

******

As Alan and his men were leaving the hidden stairway they walked right into the open arms of the police. With them were the boy's families along with Edward and Sarah. Two of the policemen kept their guns on the prisoners and guarded the treasure while two others entered the hidden stairway. A few minutes later the two boys exited the hidden stairway with shouts of joy.

"How did you know?" Hal asked.

Officer Edmunton said, "We received a call about two boys on the island being followed by some evil looking men, so we came to investigate. We were about to leave when these men exited the hidden stairway."

"But who called you!" asked Daviel.

"I did," said Edward. "I saw you boys take the shovels and pick so I watched you. I saw these men watching you from their boat so I stayed hidden. From the way they were following you I knew that they were up to no good so I called the police and everyone else."

"Officer," said Judge McKnight. "This man is Senator Mecham's son. He is wanted for kidnapping, drug dealing, drunk driving, and a hit and run accident. We will also press charges against him for tying up the boys and stealing their treasure."

"We know all about the others," said an officer. "They are two-bit hoods, always getting into trouble but it looks like this time they will be spending some time behind bars." Turning to the boys the officer asked, "May we see what is in the chest?"

"I will make a deal with you. If you promise not to tell about the secret tunnel I will show you the treasure."

"It's a deal," said the officers.

Daviel opened the chest and everyone gasped in wonder. Pulling out the dagger and crown Daviel said, "I want these. Hal, you can have the rest."

"Oh no!" said Hal. "The treasure is yours. We found it on your island. I —"

"That is true but I could not have found it if it was not for your help."

The police took the men to jail while Mr. Scott and Uncle Jim carried the chest to the mansion but not before concealing the entrance to the hidden stairway. The boys showed everyone the entrance to the secret room, the spiral stair case, the tunnel, and the cave. They put the chest of coins and jewels in the secret room. Hal took a few pieces to keep for himself.

"Dad is the treasure really mine?" asked Daviel.

"Yes, it is; the statute of limitations on this treasure would have run out many years ago. What are you going to do with it?"

Glancing at Hal he said, "After Hal takes his fair share I think I will donate it to the museum. We found Captain Smythe's treasure or at least part of it. I wonder if there is more treasure hidden on my island?"

Everyone laughed.

For more exciting adventure with Daviel, Hal, and their friends be sure to read the rest of The Daviel Amberstcrombie Series!

Book 1 The Mystery Of Crescent Hook Island

Book 2 The Mystery Of The Stolen Daggers

Book 3 The Mystery Of The Jeweled Statue

Book 4 The Mystery Of The Mysterious Stranger

Book 5 The Mystery Of The Anonymous Letters

Book 6 The Mystery Of The Crimes Of The Century

Book 7 The Mystery Of The Miscarriage Of Justice

Book 8a The Mystery Of The Missing Witness

Book 8b The Mystery Of The Phantom Seller

Book 9 The Mystery Of The Singing Mirror

Book 10 The Mystery Of Problems At The Haven

Book 11 The Mystery Of The Trail Of Bodies

Book 12a The Mystery Of The Jewel Thief

Book 12b The Mystery At Nesbit Mansion

Book 13 The Mystery of the Old Kidnappings

Book 14 The Mystery of Mirror Mansions

Book 15 The Mystery of Revenge

Other books by the Author:

The Land Of Garumph: Daniel and Scott find a spaceship in the woods. After entering the ship it takes of for the Land of Garumph, a land where animals can talk. Daniel and Scott have to save the people of Garumph from Natas who is trying to take over the planet. Can the boys save them?

Other authors published
by *Candle in the Window*

Hi, my name is Brittany Wyckoff. I live on a "farm," and much of my writing reflects the old-time values of hard work and faith in God. My books are easy reads that strive to teach you important life lessons. It is my desire that God will use my books to help you to live a life of trust and faith in Him.

I am currently writing two books:

Destry is a novel about a young man who ran away from home instead of facing his problems. But God keeps nudging him until Destry realizes that the only way he is going to have any peace is by going back home. But after five years of being gone, home is not the same. His Granny Adams, the lady who took him in, is sick and dying. In his absence, Jessica Slade has moved in to help out and has been keeping the farm going for the past couple of years. Will Destry even have a home to come back too?

Double Identity is a trilogy. Book one: Deborah has always wondered what happened to her younger sister, Magdalene, who ran off as a young teenager. But when Deborah finally meets up with her sister there's not one but two! Deborah knows that something shady is going on. She only has one sister. Deborah and Jeff have to solve the mystery surrounding them. Who would go to such lengths to make a copycat? What do they hope to gain?

Written for young adults

Hi, I'm Brianna C. Daring Wyckoff, and I was born to write! I love it. When you look for me, don't go farther than a cozy chair and keyboard. But when you visit, please bring a cup of tea. I do so love a nice cuppa accompanied by chocolate biscuits!

Taken by Mistake:

Jesse Target lives a double life. To the common citizen, he's an ordinary teenager. To a select few, he's Jesse Best—top class detective and undercover agent. His life has been anything but normal, and it only gets more interesting when a chance meeting puts him face to face with a millionaire's son who looks exactly like him.

Unraveling the mystery that surrounds his look-alike is only part of Jesse's caseload. Just as things begin to settle down with Philip Taylor, Jesse is called to go undercover to discover who is pillaging a family estate in Nevada. How is he supposed to explain his sudden disappearance to his new best friend without exposing his true, but secret, identity?

Life seldom gives downtime, and Jesse isn't allowed any. His plane has hardly landed when he receives the terrible news that Philip has gone missing.

He's vanished without a trace and Jesse can't help but wonder: Is it his fault?

Written for 13 to 16 year olds

And coming soon….

Stormology:

Surviving storms is a way of life for Javen Andrews, but when a mermaid is brought to his father's oceanic theme park, he has no idea how widespread this storm will become — or how long it will last.

Diadem never believed she'd encounter the race her people shunned long ago. Certainly she never dreamed she'd become their captive! With no allies save the quiet boy she despises, she is forced to admit she must rely on him if she ever wishes to return to her home.

Together, the pair set out to topple an empire. But when you bring down a mountain, it's impossible to dodge all the falling debris.

Written for 13 to 18 year olds

www.ingramcontent.com/pod-product-compliance
Lightning Source LLC
Chambersburg PA
CBHW070345200726
48294CB00003B/793